W9-AAT-378

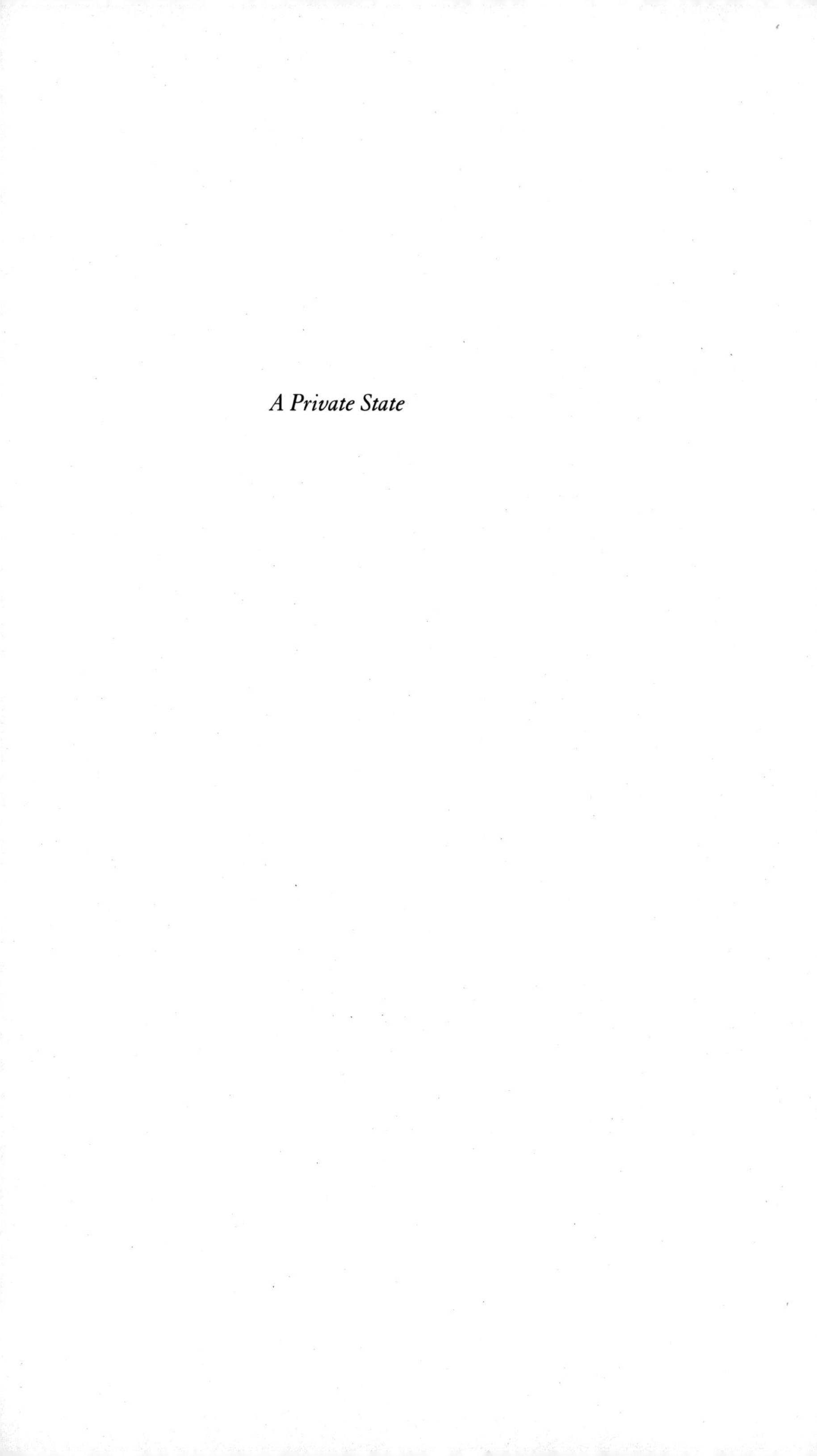

A Private State

CHARLOTTE BACON

a private state

STORIES

University of Massachusetts Press

Amherst

This book is the winner of the Associated Writing Programs 1996 Award in Short Fiction. AWP is a national, nonprofit organization dedicated to serving American letters, writers, and programs of writing. AWP's headquarters are at George Mason University, Fairfax, Virginia.

Printed in the United States of America
LC 97-14672
ISBN 1-55849-114-7
Designed by Kristina Kachele
Set in Granjon by Keystone Typesetting, Inc.
Printed and bound by Thomson Shore, Inc.
Library of Congress Cataloging-in-Publication Data
Bacon, Charlotte, 1965–
A private state : stories / Charlotte Bacon.
p. cm.
Contents: Live free or die — Arizona — Luck — A private state — Safe as houses — Pacific — Accidentals — Mercury — Monsoon — Open season — Mrs. Pritchard and Mr. Watson.
ISBN 1-55849-114-7 (alk. paper)
1. Women—United States—Social life and customs—Fiction.
I. Title.
PS3552.A27P7 1997
813′.54—dc21 97-14672
CIP

British Library Cataloguing in Publication data are available.

For my parents.

Acknowledgments

I would like to acknowledge "Other Voices" for permission to reprint, in slightly different form, "Open Season."

I would also like to thank Phillips Exeter Academy for the George Bennett Memorial Fellowship, which gave me the time and quiet needed to write or revise most of these stories.

Louise White and Rebecca Carman have my great appreciation for their patient reading and kind encouragement as the book took shape.

Finally, I want to thank Brad Choyt, who understands how important it is to try and get the words right.

contents

A Private State

live free or die

IT IS THE FIRST MONDAY OF FEBRUARY AND MARY ELLEN IS teaching George Herbert to her smartest juniors. His work is chaste but ardent and far from snowplows that wake sparks from icy streets. When Mary Ellen imagines Herbert's Britain, it is always High Summer, safe and daisied. In New Hampshire, where Mary Ellen lives, people close their faces against the cold, as if they're wary of losing warmth and moisture through extraneous talk. Then again this is New England, where talk is lean even in a lush and dappled August.

The juniors aren't, as they say, "into" Herbert, though they admire the poems where form imitates theme, such as "Easter Wings," whose stanzas seem to rise off the page like a pair of butterflies. Today, Tim, one of Mary Ellen's most pragmatic students, comments that form equals function, kind of like life.

Mary Ellen envies Tim's sturdy cheer. Last fall, her husband Frank Marten, a veterinarian who hunts, began renting across town. In December, Mary Ellen found herself wearing pale sweaters and beige pants, a snow hare in transition. Now she cloaks herself in mohair shawls the shade of ptarmigans in winter plumage. She's moving as carefully as she can through a house where she still finds flea dip in dark cupboards. Mary Ellen says, "Tim, I have to disagree. Most of the time, life has even less coherence than a smashed bug." The students eye her then, tilting back on their chairs. "Don't tilt," Mary Ellen says reflexively. But it is hard to focus on the airy hope of "Easter Wings" again.

Mary Ellen begins to explain the homework—writing a poem about anger in the shape of an arrow—when Tim's chair crashes backward. He is on the floor and screaming. "What is it, Tim?" Mary Ellen shouts. "Where does it hurt?" Then at his wrist she sees a flash of bone and blood, but his face has shrunk to something dried and crumpled, like a currant. Someone moans, "Oh Jesus."

"Jesus!" Mary Ellen repeats loudly from the floor. She turns to face the huddled students: "The nurse, I mean," she yells. "Someone get the nurse!" They don't know what she wants: Jesus, the nurse, to stay, to go. Tim's blood stains her sweater the way buckshot would pepper the chest of an unwary doe.

Magically, Tuesday is worse. The pipes at school burst and Mary Ellen creeps home to suspend her disbelief in the tub. But a steely whine is all that comes from the taps. In a haze of old habit, she finds her fingers pressing Frank's work number. Repairing damage to their home had made them feel married in some dense, authentic way. Suddenly, he's on the line and Mary Ellen freezes. "Wrong numbah," she says in an accent that floats somewhere between Maine and France. Mary Ellen is from Maryland.

"Mary Ellen?" Frank says. "What's wrong?"

"The pipes have frozen," she tells him. Talking to Frank makes her acutely conscious of the ticking of her blood. Frank hangs diagrams of animal hearts in his office, fists of muscle wrapped in festive ribbons of veins and arteries. As if hearts were weird but special gifts. Mary Ellen drops on the sofa and pulls a cushion onto her stomach.

Frank sighs. "Here, too."

"What about the animals in the surgery?" Mary Ellen sits up straight. She feels Frank is rougher than need be with domestic pets. He prefers cows and border collies in muddy barns. Working animals, not pillows with a pulse, which is what he calls creatures named Fluff and Pussums.

"We went to 7–11 and bought water for them."

Mary Ellen wants to ask if he got Poland Spring, but doesn't. She wonders who the "we" is. His assistant, Carlos Morales, nearly the only Latino in the county, is off on Tuesdays. "Mary Ellen?" Frank says.

"I don't want to know." She pulls the cushion over her head. "Just don't tell me she's seventeen."

"Her name is Dawn. And she's not seventeen." Dawn. It is remarkably close to "fawn."

Why Mary Ellen married Frank, a list Mary Ellen makes from the tub, after the plumber has visited and left her an appalling bill. Bubbles sink from peaks to flat and ratty foam.

A) He never lied: if a dog was going to die, he said, "Tiger is going to die."

B) He could build anything. They had the bluebird houses to prove it. And a hutch for black lopears, who'd escaped and mingled with the local rabbits. Summer nights, they'd wait for a half-breed, brown bodied, one dark ear coquettishly limp, to nibble its way across the yard. A little wild success.

On Wednesday, Mary Ellen receives an announcement that faculty will spend the next four Saturdays learning what to do in case of "malfunction" at the nuclear plant. As everyone within five states knows, the plant's a shaky affair, though protesters long ago stumped back home, throats hoarse. From her classroom, Mary Ellen sees the funnels of the cooling towers. It occurs to her, not for the first time, that if the plant does explode, not even Manitoba will be safe. It occurs to her safety is a relative issue.

In the faculty lounge, Mary Ellen spots a notice about training emergency-medical technicians. She immediately glances away. Cars wrapped around oak trees. Blood on windshields. Part of what is so terrible about hunting for Mary Ellen is that what's supposed to stay inside a body does not: she cannot even look at the word "appendix" in a table of contents without feeling queasy. But her eyes dart back to the flyer. She thinks of Tim in the rigid mitt of a cast. Two nights a week, the red poster says. Learn lifesaving techniques.

"Welcome to EMT-land!" Keith, the instructor, spare and brown as a winter twig, bursts into the room. Mary Ellen has never thought of traumatic injuries and their treatment as an actual destination. She imagines it as a place of gleaming ambulances, citizens with arms in tidy slings. The other students—firefighters, moms, and kids who want to join ski patrols—seem nonchalant about crossing the border from daily life to crisis management. Everyone's notebook is cracked open to the first ruled page.

Keith wears a T-shirt printed with endangered bugs despite the fact it's glacial outside and in this drafty classroom at the back of a fire station. He ticks off the topics they will cover: anatomy, CPR, trauma, poisoning, animal bites. They have to spend fifteen hours in an emergency room. In three months, Keith says blandly, they'll be ready to handle train wrecks.

There may arise an occasion when a disaster situation is so horrible that you are paralyzed and unable to respond. Do not be ashamed of those feelings, which affect approximately 20 percent of all people who are involved in such events.

EMTS in training don't start with trauma, though. They start with CPR and Little Hans, who lives in a piece of American Tourister luggage. Little Hans is a head and a chest. His mouth is slightly open and he is horribly pale, even paler than Mary Ellen and most of the other students, who, like all white people in the middle of a New Hampshire winter, have a greenish tinge. He looks depressed and northern European, something sprung from Edvard Munch.

Keith plops Little Hans on the table, so the class can see his clean, sad profile. "Now," he says, "The first step is to make sure your patient is truly unresponsive." Keith walks up to the dummy and shakes him so that all his moving parts rattle. "Little Hans, Little Hans," Keith says loudly. "Can you hear me?"

Keith goes through the motions of performing one-person CPR—he blows air between Hans's rigid lips, pumps on his sternum. The students look on earnestly, but when they've finished taking notes, their fingers press through wool and cotton to feel the bones and motion below the layers. It is impossible, Mary Ellen finds, not to make sure your own heart is still following its steady, two-step rhythm.

"ABC," says Keith, his palm on Hans's nose. "Airway, breathing, circulation. This is bread and butter for the EMT. When you don't have ABC, what you have is someone very dead." Hans appears to qualify. But what about D, E, and F? Dismemberment, eczema, flat feet. It is calming to think of all the body's problems parceled into neat groups of letters. Mary Ellen tells herself she will like this class.

But they haven't finished with ABC. Keith tells them there are some exceptions to routine attempts at resuscitation: rigor mortis, decapitation, charring, and other injuries not compatible with life. Mary Ellen knows what's not compatible with life. Husbands who date fawns. Fearing New Hampshire is permanently tilted away from the sun. Fearing your life is permanently tilted away from the sun. Mary Ellen's hands drop to her lap. G, H, I. Grand mal, hostility, inertia.

It is early Saturday evening and Mary Ellen is as usual on the phone with her younger sister Louise, a math teacher who lives in Atlanta because it's a city deeply in its region. They grew up on the Eastern Shore, in a state that wanders uneasily between the North and South: Maryland has its slave-owning past, but isn't swampily mythic enough to be truly southern. Louise likes Georgia's unequivocal heat and fatty food though she herself is trim as a nail. "Four out of five people die even with CPR," Mary Ellen tells her. "When you do it, you break ribs. You hear them crack. It's called crepitus."

"I don't care what it's called. It sounds disgusting. Hold on, I have to find my sandals." The phone falls with a thud. Louise is often dressing for a date when they talk, inching herself into pantyhose and testing lipstick colors on the back of her hand.

Mary Ellen waits and tries to imagine being warm enough to wear sandals. She doesn't try to imagine having a date. That's beyond her right now. Like her sister, she'd been in search of an authentic place and had tried to embrace New Hampshire for Frank. Five years ago, she'd imagined Yankee initiative would help her dust more often. She hasn't even swept Frank from the house yet, though she has started to toss his stray belongings into a refrigerator carton in the front hall. The box is halfway full, and late at night, she hears things inside it settle into sedimentary layers of golf balls and training leashes.

When Mary Ellen talks to Louise these days, she has more than likely wrapped herself in a huge white robe, and, if she's washed her hair, to have crowned her head in a towel. She feels then like a sinking peak of whipped cream, the kind that rapidly loses body. In this insubstantial state, her mind starts to wander.

Every morning Mary Ellen reads "Live Free or Die" on countless license plates and studies the green profile of the Old Man of the Mountains. She wonders how many people know that if the state lived up to its motto, the Old Man would die. It is thanks to massive surgery with stout wires and superglue each spring that the formation can stand the granite's shifts and swells. Otherwise he'd tumble to the bottom of Profile Lake. "Louise? Did I ever tell you the Old Man of the Mountains has wires up his nose?"

"How did we get from CPR to the Old Man?" Louise asks. "I gotta go. Glen's coming in half an hour."

Mary Ellen half-listens to Louise's rating of Glen as potential mate and partner. Louise screens her dates through a fine filter of assessment. She has turned down men because of how they set a table. She does, however, entertain tempered hopes for Glen. "Mary Ellen?" asks Louise. "Are you all right?" Mary Ellen tightens the belt on her robe and turns the three-way bulb in the lamp down to the dimmest setting. She thinks Louise goes out with men whose names sound like they could hitch themselves with ease to developments: Glenwood Pastures, Ellis Estates, Cartwright Bluffs. But Frank, what could you do with Frank? Frank Manor. Acres on the Frank. Frank has great big red hands. He could have been a butcher with those hands. He is a butcher. He hunts those fragile deer all fall. How could he look at the holes his gun tears in their necks and not notice their blood is the same color as his?

Mary Ellen can't stop thinking about the futility of rescue efforts; the crumbling emblem of her adopted state; a marriage she thought was as gray as an old steak at the back of the icebox that turned out to be fresh and bleeding after all. "Louise, we have had twelve feet of snow already this year and the deer are starving in the woods."

Louise snorts. "Stop sounding wispy. Are you eating?"

"Yes," Mary Ellen says but she doesn't say that the only dishes in her sink are bowls and spoons. She only touches food that can be served in things she can cradle to her chest. Sometimes the beat of her heart is so strong it sends a faint ripple through her soup.

That week, Mary Ellen slices her thumb nearly to the bone while opening a can of cream of tomato and thinking about Frank and his Dawn. The blood tendrils into the soup, maroon against the orange. Mary Ellen can't quite believe she's responsible for that strangely lovely blend of colors. She has suffered what her textbook would call a laceration: an incision with a neat edge. Then it starts to hurt.

Statements such as "Everything will be all right" or "There is nothing to worry about" are inappropriate. A person trapped in a wrecked car, hurting from head to foot and worrying about a loved one, knows very well that all is not right.

After EMT class one night, Mary Ellen talks with Keith about cars that provide the greatest protection during collisions. Of course he recommends the big-boned Scandinavians, hugely expensive and prone to breakdown. The next day, Mary Ellen takes out a loan and purchases a blue Volvo she names Sven.

They are lurching toward the tense goofiness of Valentine's Day when Mary Ellen succumbs to the request of her juniors to stage a reading of *Romeo and Juliet,* a play she's never really loved. How could they be so stupid to marry after meeting only once? And all those selfish adults. At least Mary Ellen insists the girls play men's parts and the boys play women's. This appeals to the students in a slightly giddy way. Besides, it is still snowing. The *Farmer's Almanac,* right on the money for the past three years, predicts storms like cold wet compresses 'til April. Sven takes the bad weather majestically.

Frank hates the winter. It keeps him indoors. They used to play Scrabble, and Frank would insist he could use medical terms. Mary Ellen let him get away with it. She made up words that looked like they had Greek roots and said they were used in prosody. Their final game, she'd achieved a splashy win using the T in "moot" to spell "disquiet." Last night, she threw the board in the refrigerator box and listened to the sharp rain of the tiles as they hit the cardboard sides.

> ROMEO: Is love a tender thing? It is too rough, too rude, / too boist'rous, and it pricks like a thorn.

> MERCUTIO: If love be rough with you, be rough with love.

The students are deep in Verona, where civil hands make civil blood unclean, but Mary Ellen's eyes keep drifting toward the cooling towers. Kimberly, plunging into Romeo's wretched farewell to Juliet, draws her back to the classroom. "Here will I remain / with worms that are thy chambermaids; O here / will I set up my everlasting rest, / and shake the yoke of inauspicious stars / from this world-wearied flesh." Kim makes a bold sweep with her sword, a metric ruler she's borrowed from Mary Ellen.

The class starts to clap and it's not even over. From the floor, Tim, as Juliet, says, "God, that's good, Kimberly."

Mary Ellen wonders if she's the only one unmoved. She tells Kim to take it down a notch or two. This is not opera. Juliet has to have his moment, too.

No one else says anything. Is she merely being crabby? Is it because she can no longer imagine anyone feeling so strung out about love? It has always bothered Mary Ellen that Romeo and Juliet don't know a damn thing about the toll of ordinary days and how that slows the pulse and grays the hair.

Tim says, sitting up, "They love each other. They can't live without each other." Kimberly flushes and tries to pull her turtleneck over her mouth. Mary Ellen notices the purple "Kimmy" on Tim's cast and the lopsided heart over the "i." There's the brink of a sneering giggle in the room that doesn't quite break out. They are all paying attention.

These days, Mary Ellen doesn't have time for love; she spends her evenings peering at bald photographs of fractures and burns. It has perhaps made her a little implacable.

"OK," she relents. "Go to town." They plunge in: Romeo and Juliet are united in death. The Capulets and Montagues relent, forgive. As the bell rings and makeshift Verona disperses, Mary Ellen hears Tim say to Kimberly, "This is so deep."

deep: pertaining to or situated inside the body and away from the skin.

Mary Ellen is talking to Louise, who is staying at home tonight with Glen, to see a movie. She'd like to ask Louise if she has ever been really aware of her heart. Did she know, for example, it was only the size of an orange? But what an orange, with its separate circuitry, its dire need for air. Instead, she tells Louise the rib cage is a poor design for protecting vital organs. Too many gaps.

Louise is silent on the line. "Do you think this class is a good thing right now?" she finally asks.

"Louise, I'm learning to revive people!" Mary Ellen says. "It's very good for me."

Mary Ellen knows Louise is feeling like she wants to see hearts as they appear on packs of cards; she doesn't want to think about the tangle of aortas and valves that thunk away in everyone's chest, even those of new boyfriends. She can understand that. The heart is so ugly really. The organ of romance and it's just dark, muscled chambers.

"What movie are you going to see?" Mary Ellen asks, propping up her turban.

The Battleship Potemkin, crows Louise. "He says it's one of his favorites." Score one for Glen. He must be lying to please Louise. No one but hoary professors of film and Louise like *The Battleship Potemkin,* could actually have watched it more than once. She hopes Glen will have the sense to keep his hands off Louise during the movie. She watches every frame.

They say good-bye. Mary Ellen turns off the dim lamp, but it is still not black enough. Mary Ellen is jealous of Louise, of the tingle of attraction she and Glen are feeling. Hand touching hand and seeing it whole. Reveling in contact.

In EMT class, Keith announces they will break into groups of three to practice binding soft-tissue injuries on Junior Hans. Junior, the size of an eight-year-old, has feet made of foam, but he sports real Keds. Red ones. Mary Ellen works with one of the firefighters and a girl who wears what Mary Ellen thinks of as a Stevie Nicks dress.

Keith shows them the assortment of plastic horrors that strap onto Hans with Velcro. There are avulsions, punctures and gunshots—entrance and exit wounds—from which to choose. The skin around the gashes does not match Junior's skin. The firefighter introduces himself as Bruce. The girl says her name is Dawn.

Dawn. Mary Ellen feels her face freeze. Frank's Dawn? She mustn't say her real name, just in case. No one in this town is double-barreled. Frank will surely have complained of some terrible intimate habit of the old wife as a sign of allegiance to the new woman. How she propped her heel on the edge of the sink to trim her toenails and that was hardly the worst. "My name is Murray," she blurts.

"Murray?" Dawn says, frowning a bit.

"Yes," Mary Ellen hears herself say. "Murray." The firefighter also looks at her.

Dawn takes Junior and smoothly attaches and binds a nasty avulsion. Mary Ellen eyes her. It is quite possible she is Frank's girl. She might not be seventeen but she's not that far past twenty. So he liked his women the way he liked his deer. Tender. "Want to try?" Dawn says to Bruce and gently passes Hans's spongy body over.

Mary Ellen toys with a gunshot wound and asks Dawn, "So what do you do?" When Dawn says that she's working part-time at a vet's office, Mary Ellen runs a hand through her hair and raises a field of static that causes several strands to levitate like nervous antennae.

For the first time, Mary Ellen understands what might push Frank to the woods with a gun. Legal annihilation. Sanctioned stalking. And underneath that, the desire to see what was once alive, wild, and inviolate opened wide and stopped.

Mary Ellen drops the wound on Junior's thigh and asks Dawn if she'd like to attend clinical observation together.

Mary Ellen starts thinking of Sven as the Fawn Tracker. She lurks in the parking lot and follows Dawn one night and discovers she is indeed living with Frank. Mary Ellen could scream at the top of her lungs inside Sven and no one would ever hear her, he's that substantial.

Questions to Ask Patients About Their Pain:
P Provokes: What brought on the pain?
Q Quality: Sharp, dull, achy, burning?
R Region: Where is the pain located?

Mary Ellen can't bring herself to tell Louise about Dawn. Her sister is too excited about Glen. Not only does he like *The Battleship Potemkin,* he wrote a master's thesis on Eisenstein. He runs a classic-film society in Atlanta. He's taking Louise to Paris for a Chaplin festival. Louise is in the grip of something big. She sounds thrilled and stiff with fear at once. It is as if she has glimpsed for sure some creature that's been rumored to live in the woods. Louise is in the woods.

The students beg to stage the playreading before the whole school. During the performance, Tybalt, a basketball player named Samantha, lunges at Romeo and hits a plywood column instead. Her sword promptly snaps in two. Tybalt, staring at her maimed weapon, cries, "Shit!"

Mercutio says, "Tybalt, thy wit is mightier than thy sword."

Later that day, Mary Ellen receives a note in her box from the principal, saying, "M.E. West: come see me re: assembly." Mary Ellen hasn't noticed in a while that her initials spell "mew."

Mary Ellen waits for Dawn at the entrance to the emergency room. "Hi, Murray!" Dawn calls cheerfully from the parking lot. "Ready?"

"No," says Mary Ellen, just as cheerful.

The E.R. smells of cotton and hydrogen peroxide, prim and almost cozy. Mary Ellen wants to report herself to the triage nurse. So soothing, that nursely touch, those pearly nails. What's the matter, dear?

Well, nurse, I suffer from jealousy so severe it's warped my liver. My husband is in love with a girl named Dawn. I am dying from Dawnorrhea.

The charge nurse, a blonde with great skin welcomes them with a pair of yellow nametags. After "Hi, my name is," Mary Ellen pauses for a moment then writes "Murray." The nurse peers at the tags stuck just above their breasts and says, "Who do we have here? Dawn . . . and Murray."

"It's her mother's maiden name," says Dawn quickly.

Mary Ellen gives the nurse a rueful smile. Dawn is smarter than her feathery hairstyle lets on. Mary Ellen wonders how much her smarts show up with Frank. He liked to be the one in charge of knowing. But maybe that has changed. Maybe love has made him a better person.

For the next few hours, it's everything from separations of the shoulder to dogs turned vicious on a master's hand. Mary Ellen remembers the stars of healed bites on Frank's palms. He treated the punctures himself, swearing and splotching his fingers with iodine. But mostly, she and Dawn see broken bones. The nurses and doctors handle the bad ankles and wrists as if they weren't quite attached to the rest of a body. "Look at this," they say and lay the injured part back down. Then there's an invitation to look at someone's cervix. Mary Ellen declines.

In the staff room, fingers laced around a cup of black coffee, Mary Ellen plans her next move. She'll lure Dawn to the house, load the box of Frank's possessions into Sven and deliver the old goods and the new girlfriend in one fine ironic swoop. In a mood of utter cool, with a slightly tilted smile, she'll appear on his doorstep, the flaps of the box neatly tucked in, and say, "Well, Frank, here are the last remains." Louise would approve. It's very Bette Davis.

"You're in luck," says a nurse. "We've got a code coming in."

"Great," says Dawn, looking sparkly after her encounter with the cervix. Mary Ellen hopes Dawn won't feel compelled to describe it. Maybe it's just the approaching heart attack that's got her happy.

"Come on, you two," says the nurse. "It's quite a show."

Mary Ellen as Murray is tucked into a corner of the trauma room, her back against the cold cylinder of an oxygen tank. She can't quite believe she and Dawn are allowed to witness such wildness in the body of someone whose name they do not even know. There's a cool, carbolic smell of medicine and, just as sharp, the stink of sweat. The patient, an elderly woman, looks as if she'd been caught in a thunder shower. Every inch of skin gleams with wet. Strands of hair curve as distinctly as scars on her cheeks. Nearly the worst is watching the body's mindless jump as the current flows from the paramedics' paddles into the chest. "Doc!" someone calls. "The nitro's not doing it." A nurse plugs another plastic tube into the IV already in the left wrist. The patient's eyes have flown open. That is the worst. They are a dark, speckled brown.

Two doctors bend to decode the EKG as it spews its spikes and valleys onto graph paper. A paramedic crouches near the monitor where the slight hills of heartbeats blip past. A professional buzz of people in soft-soled shoes surrounds the patient and her shiny gurney, her tubes, her unsteady heart. The woman's lips are flushing blue. "Doc!" a paramedic calls again and one of the doctors turns around to see what's going on.

What's going on is that the heart is giving out. Its special circuits have refused to fire. Mary Ellen and Dawn, their nametags curling slightly at the edges, stand in the corner and watch. In the woman's face, there is something wild and lost and slipping.

Frank always said he could tell when an animal was going to die. They got this look, he'd say, turning his hands palm up. Even vicious ones just lie there.

After fourteen minutes, a doctor says, "That's it. I'm going to tell the husband." A nurse gently tugs the needles from the arm, whose skin is already looking, in some small, intangible way, unalive.

At the nurses' station, Mary Ellen can see the white back of the doctor as he tells the husband that his wife has died. "I want to see Maria," they hear the man say. He comes straight to Dawn and Mary Ellen and says, "Did you see it? Did you see Maria die?"

Dawn takes the man's hand and says, "I'm sorry Maria died." Maria. Knowing her name makes it a hundred times worse. It occurs to Mary Ellen, too, that Maria is not so many letters away from Murray.

The man's hand is loose in Dawn's. It is as if he's not aware of the girl's fingers, the push of a pulse in her thumb. He says, "She was old. But she was younger than I was." It is time to go. The nurses wish them luck. The fractures keep flowing. A new shift starts. The fresh nurses unwrap the steamy layers of their coats, ask if it's been busy. The ones still on duty say no worse than usual.

Dawn's battery has failed in the cold night and Mary Ellen offers to give her a lift. She can put her Bette Davis plan into action, but feels no excitement at this idea; all she thinks is that she'll have to ask Dawn to help her with the box. They are still wearing their nametags, but Mary Ellen doesn't bother to tear hers off. Since Maria died, Mary Ellen has felt more like Murray than Mary Ellen. Having an alternate name to slip into has proved useful. It has made certain things possible.

Frank once admitted he had a totem name for himself when he hunted. A sort of secret, tribal invention. He would never tell her what it was. She understands that he was right not to speak it aloud. She doubts as well his secret name was Murray.

Dawn says she'll call a garage, but Mary Ellen tells her, "I'll take you home." She doesn't want to expose Dawn to lewd and barrel-shaped mechanics. The girl's arms are so spindly. Besides, it is snowing again and Frank will worry if she's late.

Sven revs up nicely. "Great car," says Dawn. She yawns and shivers at the same time. It is past midnight and windy. Mary Ellen tells her there's something she has to pick up at the house before she can drop Dawn off. Dawn nods. They are halfway there when the young woman says, "Murray's not your real name, is it?"

Mary Ellen agrees. "No," she says, "that's just a nickname. My real name is Juliet." A third self slips in to join Mary Ellen and Murray. Sven is getting full.

"Juliet," says Dawn. "That's pretty. You don't hear it a lot."

Dawn asks her about her family and they tell each other who was oldest and how things were. It's remarkable how comfortable it is. Mary Ellen doesn't even feel jealous anymore; she's just sort of curious. Maybe Juliet is less prone to envy.

Mary Ellen realizes, as she's listened to Dawn, that she's taken a series of wrong turns. She is on the outskirts of town, a neighborhood she doesn't often frequent, where developments replaced lumber yards, which replaced woods. Mary Ellen squints through the light haze of flakes on the windshield and sees they have just entered a community called Deer Springs. "I'm lost," Mary Ellen says. She slows the car and cuts the ignition, letting Sven's nose angle softly into a drift on the empty street. Satellite dishes, cones of snow sitting on central antennae, cast shadows the shape of angular overgrown flowers on the white lawns.

As flakes drift down, it seems to Mary Ellen she and Dawn might never get out of here. They might become a permanent fixture in Deer Springs, another thing the children could play on instead of swing sets and plastic slides in primary colors. Startlingly lifelike sculptures of a separated woman and a girlfriend. A hunter and prey. One woman on the cusp of despair, the other on the brink of voting age. There were lots of ways to look at it.

"Juliet, would you change your name if you got married?" Dawn asks her.

Mary Ellen hadn't, even with the short, tough link of a hyphen.

Marten and West, it said on the mailbox Frank had built. Brisk as lawyers. Their lives were so distinct she felt hugely betrayed when he said he had to leave because he was lonely. Didn't that just happen? Wasn't that how they'd arranged it? Hadn't it been safer like that?

"Why can't you try?" Mary Ellen had asked then.

"I have tried. I have," Frank said, as he took a buck's head from the wall. "I have," he said, stroking the muzzle. It was true. She remembers one night last winter, when Frank won Scrabble with "torque." Turning tiles to their blank side, he told her about stitching together a German shepherd that afternoon. A leg torn from a hip socket, fractured ribs, a ruptured spleen, nasty injuries. Critical, not fatal. Frank looked at the animal, the glint of his tags, the sweep of the tail, and all the bloody tangle in between and felt a strange sensation in his chest. "What's he called?" he asked Carlos.

"Fritz," Carlos said. For an instant, even knowing his name, Frank wanted to let the shepherd die. It wasn't the thought of sparing the dog a painful recovery. It wasn't that the animal was old. It was knowing he could nudge him to either side. It wouldn't have taken much, Frank said. A nick with the knife, a slight clumsiness, the heart would gush then stop. The only reason Frank picked up the scalpel and started to carve away the leaky spleen was the sight of Carlos stroking the animal's neck.

Mary Ellen hadn't known what to say then. She sat there, in the living room, drifts the size of polar bears pressing against the windows. She thinks now she murmured something about how they'd never made the word "torque" before. Maybe she'd asked if a bath would help him relax. Now she would have taken his hands and kissed them, knuckle by dry knuckle, and pulled him to their featherbed, warm and quiet in the gray light that filled their room through snowy winters.

"Yes," Mary Ellen tells Dawn. "I would change my name." She knows, too, that she has no idea what her true name might be. It comes to her, though, that it would be spelled in letters the language doesn't know. Letters that come from somewhere beyond x, y and z, ones that don't catalog the troubles that fall to doctors. Letters built from something as quick and sensitive as voltage. Letters with a charge.

"So would I," says Dawn. Sven is quiet under his fresh coat of flakes. "They'd been married forty-five years," Dawn says, and Mary Ellen sees the girl is crying. She snaps on the hazard lights, undoes her seatbelt and reaches for Dawn. As Mary Ellen wraps her arms around the girl's shoulders, a net of static crackles blue around them.

"This damn sweater," says Mary Ellen into the girl's hair. More sparks flare and die and Mary Ellen feels the wool become wet in the same place Tim's blood stained it. It would be nice to see an eight-point buck right now, sniffing and curious at the base of a satellite dish. It would distract Dawn, and Mary Ellen thinks of inventing an animal shadow so she can whisper, "Look, look!" Instead she strokes Dawn's hair and lets the damp spot on her chest grow a bit wider before asking Dawn if she's afraid of guns.

Dawn sits up and sniffles. In the glow of the hazards, she looks confused. "Of course I am." When the orange light hits the snow, it looks hot enough to melt ice, but of course it isn't.

Mary Ellen says, "Doesn't matter. You should learn to hunt. Frank would like that." She starts Sven, though at first she forgets the hazards. As she flicks them off, Mary Ellen suddenly remembers what's next for the juniors. It's Whitman. The body electric.

arizona

A GUARDRAIL—RATHER FLIMSY, JULIA THOUGHT—WAS THE only thing that kept her, Hannah, and the tourists clustered here from bouncing down the canyon's walls and into the dark river below. A Spanish family whistled and shook their heads. Mothers' hands hovered near girls with black ponytails. Julia knew the rock and grand shadows should make her feel austere and independent but in truth it only made her lonely. Even the trees out here were mavericks. A ponderosa pine to her right tilted into the ravine at an impossible angle.

But Hannah, Julia's older sister, appeared to have lived in Flagstaff long enough to be at ease with fragile edges. She'd been here a year, moving three months after their mother died of a heart attack. Hannah had recovered, it seemed. How else to read her pleasure at a horizon where a sunset the size of Rhode Island bloomed? "Did you see the swallow?" Hannah shouted above the wind.

Julia wasn't looking for birds, however; she was trying to back away from the rim. She'd imagined seeing canyons at a remove, the way she'd seen Phoenix from the air: sharply angled but mild because it was so distant. The last time she'd traveled in the West, she'd been with Hannah and their parents. Their mother bought them each a chunk of turquoise and pointed out false lakes glinting above highways. This time, Julia at least expected signs alerting her to hazards, but the notices posted were low key. No Climbing. Stay on Paths.

Nudging through the Spaniards, Julia wanted only to be back in the damp, small-hilled East. She missed the foggy mess of her greenhouse—bulbs dumped in one corner, coils of hose in another. When her mother died, Julia left her slight job in New York publishing and moved home, to the outskirts of Boston. Her father had been too numb to notice she'd taken up with plants, although her mother would have sought advice on iris, even bought a flat of pansies.

Julia thought of her father and the gin bottles piling in the trash. She thought of Henry, her new boyfriend, and his pale hands. She hadn't told Hannah about either of these things and it was nearly time to go home. Tonight, Hannah was having a party and tomorrow they'd picnic at a swimming hole. On Sunday, Julia was flying back to Boston's steaming heat.

"Look!" Hannah yelled and took Julia's arm. Julia went still, conscious of her sister's fingers on her elbow. Hannah hadn't touched her much this week. Then Julia saw the bird: the tail of the swallow against the towers of rock stretched the perspective open. Vast was the only word, a word used back East to talk about the size of debts or fortunes, not scary gaps in the earth.

Julia was about to tell her sister she wanted to go when Hannah ducked below the rail. The Spaniards muttered. Hannah turned and motioned at Julia to join her. The mothers gripped their children's wrists and bustled off, leaving the American sisters to their craziness. People always knew they were sisters—the eyes, the long, mussed hair, like neither of their parents, but quite exactly like the other. "Come on!" Hannah shouted and sat down, legs dangling.

The whole rim was rotten with dryness. As they'd walked along, they'd sent down sprays of rock, widening the canyon with their sloppy feet. "Julia!" Hannah yelled. "Don't be chicken!" Living in Arizona had smoked out Hannah's soft, eastern ways.

She didn't say please anymore and she'd acquired unusual new skills, like camping in the desert without leaving a trace.

Julia nearly shouted back, "Watch out! You were bad at the balance beam." Then she remembered that Hannah's last Christmas present was a family of three wooden armadillos, which had looked uneasy in their new home next to the schooner in a bottle. Hannah ate bulgur instead of turkey and spoke of vortices that generated healing winds. Their father drank a lot of martinis and shrank further into his chin. For him, life beyond New England already had a shimmer of unreality; he sniffed the teas and spices Hannah brought as if they might be illegal. Still, when she went back to Arizona, he said, "Hannah will miss foliage." He did not say she might miss them.

Unwinding her fingers from the guardrail, Julia wasn't sure if Hannah would be willing to admit to even remembering maples in October. Nor, when Julia called in June, had she seemed completely sympathetic to a visit. But Julia insisted. She'd just slept with Henry. She'd been having long dreams about their mother. The gin was getting worse. Julia had had a vision of herself and Hannah talking under antlered cacti in the twilight. She'd thought below the thin southwestern glaze, Hannah would still be Hannah, firmly rooted, deeply certain.

Julia eased herself down, not quite next to her sister, and became aware of the windy space below. From this perch, you could see the black river more clearly. It was dangerous out here, but Hannah leaned toward it. Julia saw that all her sister had to do was press her sneakers against the rock, gather tension in her legs, and she would tear through the sky, arms wheeling. Julia imagined Hannah dropping like a pebble in the Colorado, whose water, so dark and shining from up here, would tumble her smooth.

Then Julia realized she was the one who wanted to plant her shoes against the sandstone and fly toward the water. Maybe that would scatter the picture of their father sitting in the dark; Henry, nervous and waiting; their mother, padding to the garden. She wanted gravity pooling in her stomach and then the cleansing shock of fierce, cold water.

Hannah leaned over and said, "It'll pass. Sometimes people feel weird out here." It would have been fine if Hannah left it like that. It was actually kind. It helped Julia stop looking at the river in that mad, fixed way. But then Hannah patted Julia's knee, exactly the way their mother had to soothe a minor hurt. "Don't try and make me feel better!" Julia nearly shouted. But then wasn't that why she was visiting her sister? Because she didn't know what else to do, Julia sat there facing the wind, pushing hair from her eyes and mouth, not entirely sure if the strands belonged to her or Hannah.

Long brown hair, Julia thought later that afternoon in Hannah's kitchen. That's the only thing we have in common any more. What was this talk about *knowing* Hannah's friends? That was the excuse for tonight's barbecue. Hannah had met a lot of new people and wanted Julia to *know* them, as if the party were to last weeks as they lounged on cushions and nursed sangria. They were people from the newspaper, guys she hiked with, members of her women's group. Vivid, vegetarian and sensitive, Julia supposed. She thought of Henry's slanted smile and priestly fingers.

Julia watched her own fingers as she sliced lemons and oranges into sticky wheels. She'd nearly cut herself several times, remembering the moment on the rim which slid unaccountably into a vision of Henry's hands moving on her rib cage toward her breasts. Hannah poured bottle after bottle of Chianti into big pots, then knocked over some wine and laughed at the crimson ruin it made of the tablecloth.

Hannah had always been as neat as her name, which, if you turned it on its head, stayed the same. As opposed to what happened when Julia was flipped backward, making a sound like someone throwing up. Now Hannah laughed at permanent splotches. She'd forgotten to give Julia towels. Her nails were lined with soy-based ink from the type she used to set the headlines at Flagstaff's ecoweekly.

An unmet deadline had kept Hannah from greeting her sister at the Phoenix airport, so Julia spent the night at a hotel called the Caravanserai. The room key was attached to a tiny plastic scimitar. Julia was looking forward to telling Hannah about this, but she arrived with the newish boyfriend, Stephen. He raised his hand from the front seat in a spare way that suited his mustache. A reporter on the desert beat, he wore impressive boots.

Hannah said, "Let's get out of this cesspool," and they sped north toward Flagstaff. Julia had rather liked Phoenix, its neat streets and tired fluorescent glow. There was no air conditioning in the car—freon, Hannah explained—though that concern was a bit at odds with an old Jeep and its sizable appetite for gas. All the windows were open, which made it difficult for Julia to catch what the two in front were talking about, unless they leaned back to include her in the conversation. "Dad says hi," Julia called. He had actually said to send his love, but Julia felt uncomfortable saying "love" in such a spiky, yellow place.

Neither of them had asked her much yet, not even about the flight or if she was tired. Hannah was thinner than ever, as if all the protective layers on her body had dried out. Stephen seemed silent as a matter of policy. Maybe it helped him observe sand more closely. "When are we going to see dunes and skulls?" Julia called. "The O'Keeffe stuff?"

"She's New Mexico," Stephen said. Hannah tried to laugh. Julia sat back. She had known that. She could even spell Abiquiu. When they got to the house, Hannah said, "Now, where are you going to sleep?" and swept the books on the sofa in the study to the floor. Stephen was over every night. Julia was starting to adapt to mute breakfasts of kasha with goat's milk.

Hannah was working, so Julia tried to occupy herself in the

backyard. But the stiff tangles of sagebrush didn't need a lot of ministration. Julia was used to delicate nets of roots, but plants out here were more like weapons than ornaments. She ventured into Flagstaff instead, where she could sharpen her spurs or buy a crystal to purge grief. Mormon missionaries prowled about on sleek, thick-tired bikes. Several approached her as she sat over iced tea.

Henry would have enjoyed talking to the Mormons. Julia had met him at the nursery, where he came to purchase hyacinth for the beds in front of his church. He was a Lutheran vestryman. A number of Christians bought their gardening supplies there, but Henry was the only one who said thank you instead of God Bless, which was the first thing she'd noticed. Then she'd seen the band of gold on the usual finger. But the ring hadn't kept him from asking, a week later, struggling to keep his grip on a bag of peat moss, if he could buy her coffee. The whole thing—Henry's car parked blocks away, shades pulled mid-afternoon—made Julia feel soiled and adult in a dark, impractical way.

She'd never have gotten wound into something like this if her mother were alive. Her parents, still at ease in marriage after thirty years, without saying a word rejected anything but calm and thoughtful union. Soon after the coffee, Julia lost her shears in the roses, misplaced her license, bounced a large check. Her boss peered at her and said, "You're happy, I think." That night Julia asked Hannah if she could come see her.

But the most personal topic Hannah had broached was asking if Julia knew an organic way to keep slugs off basil. Julia told her to pour beer into yogurt lids and put them around the plants. "Do they die?" Hannah said. "Isn't there something less drastic?" Julia said testily beer was hardly malathion. You choose, Hannah, she said, slugs or basil. That hadn't gone over well. Julia went off and wrote a letter to Henry in which she tried to sound enthusiastic about the lack of humidity out here in the True West.

But she ended up shredding the whole thing and flushing it down the toilet, which promptly clogged.

"A good purge, that's what I need," Julia thought that night as she poked a tortilla shard in the bean dip. She went to sit on the arm of Hannah's sofa and glanced around the crowded living room. Why hadn't she brought brighter clothes? Her black sundress, chic and understated in Boston, looked all wrong out here. Everyone else had on shirts and pants in sunset reds and yellows. Even the piñata, a stocky burro swaying from the ceiling, wore a purple saddle.

The smell of grilling vegetables wafted through screens. The sangria had been popular. Julia's glass had been filled and emptied several times, which kept her from conversation with the hawk-lonely teetotalers studying to be shamans. Others had tried to make more contact. Several members of the women's group had taken both of Julia's hands in theirs and squeezed. "Julia," they said. "Welcome." Other guests exclaimed how much she and Hannah looked alike then drifted off, in the way of all parties, no matter how evolved the guests.

Hannah was talking to a man about a school-board election. Others were arguing about how to block zoning for a Wal-Mart. Local, insular talk. Julia, if anyone had asked, might have mentioned that she encouraged the sale of native plants. That she was living in the same town she grew up in, unlike any of these people drying out from too much toxic time in L.A. or New York. Someone put mariachi music on the stereo. The piñata began to jiggle. Couples whooped and started to dance.

Julia went to the study, taking with her a pitcher of sangria and a tall yellow candle. Its rim had melted into a scalloped edge that made it look like one of the nursery's fanciest tulips. She held it close to Hannah's desk and looked at photos. Hannah on a pinto, holding the pommel with a casual hand. Hannah linking arms with women gleeful at their conquest of a bald peak. Not a single picture of her sister in any phase but Arizonan. Waxy drops rolled to the desk. The door swung wide and Julia turned to see Stephen. "Having fun?"

Julia looked at him and said, "Oh yes. Tons."

He closed the door and stretched out on the sofa, rumpled with Julia's sheets, and said, "What did you think of the canyon?"

"Impressive." She gestured vaguely, hoping she'd lit on the right word.

He wandered over to the wine and poured himself some more. "You never get used to it," he said. "You just feel sort of small out here all the time." It was the only thing he'd said yet that made her like him.

"But Hannah loves it," Julia said and sat down at the desk.

Stephen sat nearby and said nothing, which felt fine, not awkward. The whole-grain breakfasts had accustomed them to pauses. The floor rang with music. "Hold on," he said, and went to the living room. He came back with chips and guacamole. "I like this stuff."

"Me, too," said Julia. She thought avocados were beautiful, their flesh sliding quietly from green to white at the pit. Even more, she liked mashing them for Henry, whose wife thought they were too fattening to have in the house. She had realized instantly, as the fork met the soft slices, that this was competition. "Henry likes it, too."

"Is he your boyfriend?"

"I think so," she said.

"New?"

"Married."

"Complicated," said Stephen tranquilly.

So Julia started to talk to Stephen, and it tumbled from her like gardener's twine unraveling from a badly wound ball. But listening to the story out loud for the first time, she was sad to hear how common it seemed, and she stopped. Partly it was how brittle

Henry's name sounded in the dry air. But mostly, it was realizing she was telling the wrong story. What she really wanted to say was that she was having dreams about her mother so real she woke up sometimes thinking she could smell her skin. Stephen poured more wine and said, "You ever cut your hair?"

Julia shook her head no. The three longhaired women. My Rapunzels, her father called them.

"Can I do it?" he asked. "Short?"

"OK," she heard herself say.

Stephen wet a comb in the bathroom, shifted his chair closer to hers, and wrapped a towel around her neck. Then he eased out the scissors on his Swiss Army knife. "You're going to use those?" Julia asked.

"Don't worry. I got the best haircut of my life with them." He turned on a small lamp. The comb slid across her scalp. He went straight to the base of her skull and a skein of hair fell to the ground.

"Stop!" Julia said, clutching her head. "Just a minute." She remembered how Henry loved to braid her hair. She remembered even better her mother brushing it smooth for school. But these were things that couldn't be allowed to make a difference anymore. He might as well go on. "OK," she said. He snipped slowly, his breath steady. A damp mass of brown slid into her lap. They were quiet for a minute. The candle guttered out. Julia asked him, "Do you love Hannah?" She'd given him permission to cut her hair and felt entitled to some large, abrupt questions.

Stephen stopped. "Love. Wow. Big word." The scissors started again. "Do you?"

"Of course," Julia protested.

"Just because she's your sister, you don't have to."

"Everyone's so groovy out here," Julia heard herself saying. "If you don't feel like being nice, that's OK, you're just in a bad space. What's bad space, anyway," Julia said, a little louder. "Some cave where you put the meat eaters?"

"Sit still," said Stephen. "I'm going to mess up the line."

"How come losing your temper out here is a federal crime?" Julia said, sitting up straight. "How come Hannah makes me feel like a serial killer when I tell her how to get rid of slugs? She's murdered plenty of insects. Mosquitoes eat her alive."

Stephen laughed and said, "Not many of those in Flagstaff. Too dry."

"Do you know what Hannah did when she lived back East? She wrote corporate newsletters," Julia said, smacking the desk.

"No wonder she wanted to come out here," Stephen sighed.

Julia really wanted to ask him if he knew about their cat, their mother and her garden. Did he know that Hannah got the hook-shaped scar in her arm from the old Persian? That their mother told Hannah it was her own fault: Hannah knew how grumpy the cat was. Did he know stories like that? Then Julia let it cross her mind that Henry wasn't all that comfortable either with talk of surly pets or parents.

"She's happy here," Stephen said. "For the most part." Julia listened for more, but he didn't go on.

"Does she ever talk about me? About when we were little?"

"Not really." He took the plant mister from the windowsill. Spray settled on Julia's cheeks in a fine net.

"Not ever?" What caught Julia by surprise was that learning this was the most painful news of all.

"Settle down," he said and straightened the towel on her shoulders. "Talk to Hannah. She's the one making you mad." He started cutting again.

"Hannah doesn't want to talk to me." Julia's throat felt tight. She picked up a foot-long piece of hair. "I don't want to see," she said. "Get some tape. Put it back." She put her head between her legs.

"Come on, close your eyes." He led her to the bathroom. Air tickled her neck. Stephen squared her shoulders and said, "Look." She saw two dark eyes framed by chin-length hair. A new face.

Half of Stephen's smile reflected in a corner of the mirror. "Hold on," he said and clipped a few strands. "Well?" His hand was warm on her nape.

Then Hannah was there, the noise of the hot, winey room rushing in behind her. Her hair had slipped from its chignon and tendrilled down her back. "Come on, they're doing the piñata," she called. "My God. You let him cut your hair. It looks great," she said, coming into the bathroom. Julia watched her sister's face and saw that Hannah was struggling not to be jealous.

When the guests saw Julia, a collective hoot went up. "All *right,*" they cried. "Baby!" someone shouted. A pair of hands pulled her and Hannah to the center of the circle below the piñata, spinning from the last blow. Paper shingles of the burro's skin floated down on the sisters. Hannah went back to Stephen and wound herself onto his arm. But Julia stood there while someone took another whack. A hollow leg fell off. "Harder," someone yelled. The burro's side caved in and a thin spill of foil-wrapped candy trickled out. Julia stood below, hands spread wide, because it seemed important to try to hold some of the slippery treasure.

Waking the next morning with the sun slanting across her bed, Julia felt for the first time the West might have possibilities. She unwrapped one of the piñata candies and lay in bed, letting the bitter chocolate melt on her tongue. The day was shatteringly clear. At breakfast, Stephen said, "It was great how everyone liked your haircut." Julia poured more goat's milk on her cereal. She was starting not to mind its sour edge.

Hannah was busy with pots at the sink. "Stephen, I want to leave for the swimming hole at ten."

"I'm not going, I don't think," he said, stretching his long arms.

"You're not? Why?" Her hair today was pinned in a severe bun.

He had work to do, he said. Hannah frowned until he kissed the top of her head. "Adios," he waved to the sisters.

"I'd still like to go," Julia said. "Let's clean up later." But Hannah wouldn't leave until she'd swept away all the scraps of the piñata, whose two front legs, not quite severed, tilted from the trash can.

By the time they arrived, the light had changed. "Looks like rain," Julia said, not knowing if this were accurate or not. Something in the air smelled different. It might have been moisture.

All week, Hannah had talked about her picnic grove in the gorge. There were waterfalls, she said, and high cliffs where the Anasazi had likely lived. The way Hannah described the place, Julia expected sacral hush. Instead there was a rutted space where people parked trucks with huge wheels. Yowls filled the air, noise that came from the first pool, brimming with boys in rooster-bright shorts jumping from ledges in the sandstone cliffs. The water burst up white as their bodies slammed into the pool. Julia wondered what the Anasazi would have thought of that. Hannah disapproved. Though sunglasses shaded her eyes, her mouth thinned. Julia thought the Indians might have enjoyed the wildness of the leaps, the immersion. "Looks like fun," Julia said.

Hannah looked at her squarely. Julia had never been good on a high dive and Hannah knew it. But instead of challenging Julia to try the jump, Hannah murmured there'd be fewer people upstream. She was wrong. Swimmers lined the banks of every spot deep enough to wade in. On a sandy spit, in the shade of a willow, she finally said, "This looks like it."

Julia stripped off her shoes, eager for the tingle of deep water, but the river was warm. Weeds flowed along the bed. Triangles of broken bottle were scattered on the bank. Hannah settled her things, then unpinned her bun. Seeing the glow of her sister's hair, Julia felt the sudden lack of her own. "This is where Stephen and I come. During the week when no one's here."

Julia could imagine them making love on the sand, under the gauzy screen of willow leaves. Julia thought of the stuffiness of the afternoons she spent with Henry, how he made sure all the windows were closed so no one could hear them. Then two girls appeared on the opposite bank, below the cliff. They were fourteen or fifteen, hips and thighs already ripe, rippling. Their wet tops clung in bubbles to their skin. Giggling, fleshy, sad, they held chips of rock and turned to the cliff to scratch hearts. Julia looked at them etching the empty curves. Given the chance, she might have been tempted to add one herself. But her sister was fuming beside her. "Don't, Hannah," Julia said. "Let them be." Don't you remember, Hannah, she wanted to ask, the letters we carved in the birch with steak knives? Don't you remember how Mom slapped us?

Julia stared carefully at the way the sun lit the angled edge of the broken glass by her hand, then looked up at the girls filling the hearts with initials and ampersands. Those marks would wash off; the birch was still mending. "Do you wish I hadn't come?" Julia asked and stood up. Hannah said nothing. "I have to tell you I don't think your boyfriend is the nicest guy."

Hannah snapped, "I hear you've taken up with a married man." Suddenly, they were both standing.

"If I'd let him, Stephen would have kissed me," Julia shouted.

The girls stopped scratching and stared. "In your dreams," Hannah shouted back.

In her dreams, Julia wanted to scream at her sister, all she saw was their mother, braid bouncing as she wandered the house. Instead, she ran at Hannah and pushed her backward into the water. The girls fled. Hannah's dark glasses flew off. Her arms flailed, the way they had when she'd first learned to swim. Julia had always been better in water. She waded into the pool, stones and weeds slipping under her feet. She reached a hand toward Hannah, who grabbed it hard, pulling Julia in on top of her.

They splashed in the dead center of the pool, spouting, trying to gain a foothold. It was colder out here than Julia expected, cleaner feeling. They started to push toward the shore, breathing hard, bodies half in water, half in air. Hannah's hair tangled in a wet, black root straggling down her back. Julia's was drying fast against her cheek. But even in their stumbling, anyone could see they were related, arms tilting just the same way as they tried to balance themselves. As they reached the bank, they looked at each other, motherless, motherless.

"DUNCAN'S GONE," LILLIAN TOLD OWEN. SHE WAS STANDING in the driveway, wearing garden gloves and holding a trowel streaked with dirt.

"He's probably seducing that retriever around the corner," Owen said and hauled his briefcase from the backseat. "Unless of course he's upstairs reading Tolstoy."

"Tolstoy. For God's sake, Owen," Lillian said, though the retriever was an idea. They ought to have had the stupid corgi neutered as a pup. But Lillian phoned the golden's owner and found that a minivan had killed the poor dog last week. "Emma's been run over," she told her husband, who'd come into the kitchen, one hand wrapped mid-stem around a glass, the other trailing the day's mail.

"Bombing started in Sarajevo again," Owen answered. When he hadn't heard her, he sometimes offered summaries of the day's dark events. The raw troubles of the Balkans, already unreal in the southern wedge of Connecticut, were even less believable in the slow light of May. In May, Lillian tossed the sad, fat sections of international news unread in the trash. But tonight, with Duncan gone and Emma dead, Lillian's mind filled with the vision of a woman sprawled in an alley, the frothy greens of carrots spilling from her basket.

"Emma was left for hours on the road," Lillian said, slightly louder. On the counter sat a can of Duncan's food. Next to it, a head of lettuce flopped against a pair of chicken breasts they were going to have for supper.

"Don't fret, Lillian. How far can a ten-year-old corgi wander?"

"Miles, for all I know," Lillian muttered, putting down the trowel and washing her hands.

"He'll be back," Owen said and slipped a statement from its sheath. "When's the last time you saw him?"

"About fifteen minutes ago. I was weeding, he was there, you know, lolling and panting. Then he wandered out front and when I called he didn't come." Lillian realized then she didn't believe in instantly replacing a pet, as she'd urged Emma's owner to do. It wasn't as simple as deciding the guest room needed fresh curtains.

She looked at Owen. It was 6:30 and Duncan was out there when he should only be here, tangled in her feet, crazy for scraps, and there was Owen deep in some plea from a phone company. Lillian was going to find her dog. She tucked her shirt in tighter and said, "Owen, get the chicken ready, will you? I'm going to look for Duncan."

"Stop fussing. He's out eating someone's trash," Owen said, not looking up from the advertisement.

"I'll just check around the block." She couldn't dislodge the picture of the woman in the alley, the brown kerchief, the basket's tight weave.

"Lillian," he said and looked up. "Stay put." The mail sorted, he wanted to talk, about the lateness of the 5:09, the pollen count, the Serbs. Talk to fill the blue bowl of the evening, while that poor fat dog waddled across streets, testing his blind luck.

"Four minutes both sides," Lillian said. In the garage, she grabbed a box of dog biscuits, then drove slowly through the neighborhood, calling for Duncan through the open window. As she rolled past the neat houses, it struck her how few people they knew here now. Their oldest neighbors, Bob and Claudia Merchant, had moved last month to Chapel Hill. Did that make

Lillian and Owen the unconsulted historians of the area? Objects of musty, bored respect, the kind reserved for cousins many times removed? More likely they had no role at all. "Duncan!" Lillian called, rather more loudly.

A pair of boys were the only ones to answer. They looked much like Lillian's children had, hooting through the dusk on newly mastered two-wheelers. It was soothing to know nine-year-olds still understood the panic of losing things as iconic as pets or fossils found on mountains. But her kids' pockets were lumpy with marbles, not beepers. The boys darted ahead, whistling down streets Lillian had hardly ever noticed, broadcasting Duncan's loss. Then an electronic chirp sounded in the twilight and they told her they were sorry but they had to go.

Lillian turned the car around, steering past a Victorian that a young couple had restored to perfect, ghostless fussiness. Lillian had met the wife at the vet's, their expensive cat coiled inside its carrier. She thought now she should call the vet to see if anyone had reported an injured dog. From a phone outside a new all-night pharmacy, Lillian told the receptionist that Duncan the old corgi was missing. Of course he was licensed. He wore a name tag, too, green and heart-shaped, Lillian admitted. "Do you think he's been stolen?" she asked. The woman sighed.

Lillian drove back past the Victorian and saw in the floodlight the woman waiting in the door for her husband, just returned from work. Two shadows, one perched, one in motion, anticipating contact. Lillian wondered when it was, exactly, that she found more pleasure stroking the notched, velvet thinness of a dog's ear than her husband's back.

It hadn't always been like that. Lillian let herself recall the last time she'd spent the evening in a car, driving about the neighborhood in fruitless sadness. It was just over ten years ago, and she'd recently discovered she was pregnant. Forty-six and pregnant all because the boys, launched at their serious schools, had left the house in pale-blue stillness. Lillian and Owen had started to bump into each other in the midst of Saturday's most ordinary chores and found themselves, despite topsoil under nails and a frieze of just-cut grass on pant legs, dissolved to uselessness with lust.

They made love everywhere, pausing to close curtains but not to search for birth control. In the den, on the living-room rug, bifocals thrown carefully clear. Owen's ankles printed with ribs of tennis socks, the skin of Lillian's back dented where bra hooks pressed, light spread across their lumps and scars, the folds and puckers of bodies that had slipped, almost without their knowing, past their prime. Lillian opened then shut her eyes, not quite ready to admit the extent of the change but almost excited for the release from pride.

Slightly aroused, if abashed, Owen led her to bed when she told him the news. Afterward, Lillian had asked, "Do we have to?"

Owen propped himself on an elbow. "Do we have to what?" When she stayed quiet, he looked harder at her and said, "You can't be serious."

She sat up and took a pillow to cover her breasts. "I might be," she said. What a chance to blur the picture of the years ahead. The huge, unsteady luck of a child.

He pulled the pillow from her body and said, "Lovey, be reasonable."

"Why?" she'd asked, but he hadn't answered. It was then she'd thrown on her clothes and bolted out of the house and into the car. Down their street of white clapboard and black shutters, then along roads named after brooks, soon to be polluted. At last she'd found herself in a development, staring at a bulldozer whose scoop was caked in earth, peering into the cellars of houses yet to be built.

The next day, on her knees in phlox that sprouted far beyond its bed, Lillian felt a quick spread of dampness between her legs. The stain in her pants rinsed easily away. Wrinkled, soapy trousers and underwear dripping in the sink, she stood in front of the mirror. It was a beautiful day and the light showed every line in her face. "It feels awful," she said to her reflection. That week, without asking Owen, cramps still twisting her belly, she bought Duncan. She chose him for the lightness of his bite. The milky needles of his teeth hadn't even dented her skin.

Tonight, ten years later, the kitchen was quiet and smelled heavily of old dog. Owen had shut himself up in the library, from which Lillian heard the dull and stately rhythms of public television.

A frog, throat bulging to a veined bubble, filled the screen. Its skin was deadly to the touch, the British announcer droned, as if the English had taken lethal frogs in stride centuries ago. Owen was deep in a book, a tall blond glass of whisky on the table. When she'd told him about the miscarriage, he'd covered her with fast, firm kisses, but their touches had grown more cautious since. They'd started reading classics aloud, and bed had gradually become a place for cool, still sleep. "I couldn't find him," she said. "What are you reading?"

Owen flashed the cover: a paperback of the Brothers K. Bad signs, immersion in the half-light of scotch and Dostoevsky, though there were ways to turn the evening's luck. She could have asked, for instance, if Dosto's wife loved him as much as people said. But Owen shifted his legs as if he were stiff and said, "Lillian, he's an old dog. Maybe he wandered off the way elephants do. Maybe all he wants is peace." Amphibians, hooch, tortured Russians, Lillian thought. If that was peace, he could have it. It looked more like a deep sulk.

In the bedroom, she watched shows on the small TV until the news came on. She didn't need to learn any more about besieged cities and dying women. They were all floating around somewhere in the night, them along with liquored-up husbands and Duncan, knocking over garbage cans and barking at leaves. Such a stupid, easy life. Why had he drifted away from it now? All night, she heard Owen downstairs, bumping into furniture, looking for what she didn't know.

He came to the bedroom early the next morning, already packaged for the city in his tie and overcoat. "I forgot to tell you. I've got a breakfast meeting. Good luck with the dog." Thick with sleep, Lillian barely heard her husband. The pillow smelled of flea collar and pine, Duncan's smell. He hadn't woken her for the first time in years. She felt guilty for being able to rest at all.

Making coffee, Lillian remembered the vet's assistant had suggested one of those terrible posters. Telephone poles and bulletin boards layered in announcements of jobs available and sofas for cheap, as if a lost dog were remotely equivalent to the sale of a three-piece sectional.

Still, Lillian found herself driving at 8:45 to the Xerox shop with a picture of the dog she had taken last Christmas. It was blurry, Lillian never being very good with cameras, which were left to Owen and the boys, silently, profoundly, absorbed in all things technical and geometric. In the snapshot Duncan wore a wide green ribbon.

The man at the counter blinked at his customers from behind glasses as round as a pair of full moons. He himself might have been the moon, he was that spherical and pale. But no, Lillian thought, he reminded her more of a grounded cloud. His name tag said "Let me help you. I am JIM P." The capitals suited him.

"Hello," Lillian said, "Do you think this photo will Xerox all right?"

Jim examined it and Lillian felt a pang of discomfort showing this stranger her dog. For a moment, she saw Duncan as others must: eyes silver with cataracts, ears and rear end too large. She wanted to snatch the picture from Jim's dimpled hand and cry, "He's mine, at least, he's mine."

But Jim said, "What a great dog. He's got a kind of wit about him."

"Yes," Lillian said, "That's it! That's just it!" That was just the word. Duncan was dry in his ploys to steal and bury shoes and tennis balls. She explained she needed the copies because he was missing.

"Well," sighed Jim. He confessed that his Siamese, Pitiporn, had just died.

"Pitiporn?" Lillian asked. Name of a ducal family in Thailand, Jim explained.

"Ah," said Lillian. "How sad."

"Great cat," he said somberly. "She was an absolutely great cat." He suggested orange paper for Lillian's flyers. She agreed to the bright color, but decided against the personal appeal from the dog. Last week she'd seen an embarrassing poster that said, "Hi My Name is Kelp. I'm A Much-Missed Chocolate Lab." Lillian's text stressed "Reward" instead, as if kidnappers were waiting greedily for posters decked with dollars. When she offered a twenty, Jim raised his palm and said quietly, "On the house today."

Lillian smiled her thanks, not trusting herself to speak, and headed out to the parking lot. The light today was lovely, even for heading off to post notices of a lost and ragged dog in malls built on land that once belonged to dairy farms. It occurred to her today those old fields might have been such a violent green thanks to some pesticide people liked to use back then.

At a bagel bakery where she taped a sign, the cashier asked what had happened. Lillian said her dog was gone. The signs were in case he didn't find his way back.

"You mean he's going to come home all by himself?" Lillian saw the girl's tag said her name was Kris.

"I know it sounds odd," said Lillian, "but they have a tremendous instinct for it."

"In their little dog hearts they just know?"

It was true, Lillian protested. As a girl, she'd had a dog who walked twenty miles along a highway to come back to her. She'd forgotten this 'til she told Kris, but it had actually only been five.

"Loyalty," said Kris, seeming impressed. "That's wild. But why would he leave?"

"Someone took him," Lillian said, "right from the yard."

"Hmm," said Kris. She had a shock of goldfinch yellow hair

that came, as people used to say, from the bottle. A dab of cream cheese partially masked the K on her name tag. Duncan rarely just wandered off, Lillian explained. Perhaps a child who'd seen him decided to take him home. When the parents saw the posters, they'd return the dog. This was one of the stories Lillian told herself under the comforter last night. It sounded even thinner in fluorescent light, lox and hazelnut in the air.

Kris picked up a plastic knife and smoothed the surface of a bucket of margarine. "You have too much respect upon the world: they lose it that do buy it with much care," she said to the knife, clearly quoting. It had to be Shakespeare, but all Lillian could do was smile and hope she looked knowing and appreciative. Kris loaded some day-old bagels in a sack. "Here," she said, thrusting the bag into Lillian's arms. "I hope my instincts are wrong."

That evening, Lillian told Owen "I put up signs all day, I found out our taxes pay for a road-kill officer, I plugged in that answering machine and nothing." They were in the kitchen, and though it was late, neither had eaten. Lillian dusted some web from the machine, which had once belonged to the boys. "You're sweet, but our dance cards aren't that full," she'd said and waved the contraption away as if it were a wasp, the same gesture she'd used to reject microwaves and computers, also offered secondhand. Today, she'd rescued the machine from the attic and spent an hour deciphering instructions before the red eye began to blink.

Well launched on a bottle of Soave, Lillian rambled about Jim P. and Kris, the quoting girl, the false intimacy of nametags. Rooting in a cupboard, Owen came across the bagels. "Shakespeare?" he said and looked inside the bag. "What are these doing here?" he asked, holding up a poppy-studded roll. Owen and Lillian had moved from New York at a time when bagels were still ethnic food. Their breakfasts were white toast, bacon, black coffee, a meal from another century.

"The quoting girl gave them to me. Do you recognize this?

There was something about having too much respect for the world and losing it."

Owen chewed some bagel. "*Merchant of Venice*" he said after a minute. "You have too much respect upon the world: they lose it that do buy it with much care. Hah!" he said, pleased. "Why was a girl in a bakery quoting Shakespeare?"

"I don't know," Lillian said. She was abruptly exhausted. She was thinking that she would die if she couldn't scratch the roll of skin on Duncan's neck soon. That Owen and some sad girl at a mall were probably the last two Americans to soothe themselves with great, old books. That more shells had fallen in Bosnia today. She'd read the headlines in spite of herself. Picking up the paper from the stoop, she'd also seen Emma's owner crossing the street, gray in the face, wearing one pearl earring.

"I'm not cooking," Lillian said forcefully and tipped the last drops of wine into her glass. "Twelve people were killed in a Muslim safe area today."

Owen had undone his tie. "We could go to that Italian joint," he said.

But they might miss a call from someone who'd seen Duncan.

"Lillian," Owen said, putting down his bagel, "no one's going to call."

"Owen!" Lillian cried, pounding the counter. The bagel fell to the floor. "How do you know that?" She picked up the roll, gray with lint and dog hair, and to their mutual surprise, threw it hard at Owen, who, with a wildly lucky grab, just kept it from shattering his wine glass.

Lillian was sorry it hadn't broken. "I'm not cooking," she said again and thumped up the stairs. Once there, she didn't know what to do with herself. After pacing the hall, she decided to take a bath to escape the framed family photos. She turned on the tub, plopped into the steamy water, and, recalled the early months of her first pregnancy. She and Owen were living in New York and the city had seemed to swirl with germs and trouble. She remembered jackhammers pummeling a sidewalk to dust as she cradled her stomach and thought, I need a home, and the vision that came was of doors with locks and gates that closed with a solid clack of metal.

Just before Andy was born, they'd chanced onto this house and Lillian entered twelve years of frankly housebound domesticity. Broken bones and parts denied in plays had seemed lapses of luck. Once Owen got fired. Friends divorced; there'd been untimely cancers. Much had made her sad: bombs on Cambodia, lying presidents. A niece, pretty and wayward, dead of heroin at twenty-two. But even looking up from tulips and seeing America gone star-crossed never really made her worry that Arnold's bread would not get baked or well-trained dogs not come when called.

Soaping her arms, she wondered what childhood in this soft place had really done to her sons. They'd become implacable adults: tall, employed, at ease with hard drives and work that required more time on airplanes than land. If they were nervous about their prospects in this chancier era, they didn't tell Lillian. They had words for everything. Even not having a job for a spell was called rethinking their options. Every situation could be coaxed to yield good fortune.

She should feel lucky to have raised such solid children. But tonight, floating in the warm water, wondering where the dog had gone, she couldn't stop remembering when gravity first became her children's ally. "Get off that bike now or I will pull you into the house myself," she'd told John soon after he turned ten. Hannah, the corgi before Duncan and sensitive to family upset, was barking her head off.

"I won't," he screamed. Lillian marched over, dragged him off the bike and abruptly became aware she could not hold this squirming mass of boy whom 'til now she'd been able to move as if he weighed no more than a pachysandra.

He broke from her arms and ran to the overturned bike, whose wheels spun and clicked. "I hate you!" he shouted. The spokes were sharp and silver in the evening light. Hannah had turned her snout to the sky and howled. Who are my sons? Lillian wondered, clean arms lying on the water, remembering how the glints off the spokes had pierced her.

Gravity also did terrible things to skin, she thought, looking at her hands, and drinking did terrible things to memory. The wine retrieved the boys, then Hannah, and now she missed both sons and two old dogs. Her thinking blurred with children and old pets, she was angry with herself for never letting the boys know how sharply the world could crack, how women, animals, and children could fall inside. Women in Sarajevo didn't have to say a word about that. Women there knew all about the fact that books read, money saved, and azaleas planted couldn't save you when, for no earthly reason, your luck just blew away. Bombs in market squares did the work for them. Duncan, Lillian knew, was really gone.

She was floating in the now-cool water when she heard Owen call, "Lillian! Phone!" She hadn't even heard the ring. The air struck her wet skin and the towel barely covered her body. Oh, I've faded, she said to herself. I'm a fat old woman now. Dripping a wide circle on the bedspread, she picked up the receiver. Owen was on the kitchen extension. "Hello?" she said.

"All right!" an unfamiliar voice answered. "Everyone here? Hey, did you know your machine's not working?" This was said in a rather accusing way, though casually. The accent was not of the East.

"Who is this?" Lillian said, holding the phone firmly.

"Holly Allen. I'm calling from the Grand Junction Animal Shelter? We've got a corgi here named Duncan who'd probably like to talk you."

"Colorado?" was all Lillian could say. "What's he doing in Colorado?"

"Good Lord," said Owen.

"He just came in. One of our animal-control officers found him on Route 70."

"Is he all right?" Lillian found herself shouting. "What happened to him?"

"Lower your voice, Lillian," Owen said.

"No clue, but he's fine," Holly said, still casual. "Where's this I'm calling anyway?"

"Connecticut," Owen said faintly.

"Wow," said Holly. "Hey, Duncan, want to say hi to your parents?" Lillian heard a rustle that could have been someone rattling papers into a neat sheaf. "Hey guys," Holly called to her colleagues, "the corgi's from Connecticut." Then she asked, "Folks, is he on any medication?"

Lillian couldn't answer. She was picturing Duncan's nose stuck out the window of a stranger's car, ears pinned flat with speed. Duncan trundling along the shoulder of a highway that shone with broken bits of windshield and dead crows. Duncan safe. Why, Lillian wondered, clean and cold and dripping, why am I disappointed?

Two days later, she told the baggage attendant at the airport, "I'm here for my dog." He led her to a dim room that smelled of cardboard and diesel fuel. His overalls had "José" stitched into a pocket. "This your little guy, ma'am?"

"Yes, he's mine, José," Lillian said and felt, for the first time since she'd known Duncan was returning, a solid thrill of pleasure. "Duncan," she called and then he was in her arms, a bundle of old-dog claws and tongue and tail. She held him at arm's length and looked at him, the same brave, rare way she'd looked at her own face in the morning light just after losing the baby. How awkward he was, such bowed legs, cataracts milkier than ever. What catastrophic breath. How she loved him.

José asked, "So what happened here?" Duncan in her arms, Lillian told the attendant about the disappearance, the making of signs, the call from Colorado. The thief hadn't bothered to remove his tags. José took off his gloves and said, stroking Duncan's head, "You are one lucky dog. Why you, little guy? Who you got looking after you?" Duncan breathed his terrible breath into the small room. "Why you?" José said again.

In the car, the dog in the front seat, nose glued to the vent, Lillian asked herself the same question. Why Duncan? José had said, "I don't know about you, but I detect some divine intervention here." Lillian thought the sky looked too calm for God, too bland for anything but the occasional plane, sparrow, or column of pollution. At least she could thank Jim and Kris and get rid of those signs.

But Kris had quit, the bagel manager said. Lillian asked for a forwarding address. Kris was a friend. The manager gave Lillian a glance as if trying to assess the likelihood of a bond between someone with a haircut like Kris's and a woman with a handbag like Lillian's. He said it was against policy to give out personal data on employees. "But she doesn't work here anymore," Lillian pointed out. The policy extended to former workers, too, he added. "Well," said Lillian and haughtily bought a tub of scallion cream cheese.

She took Duncan with her into the copy store and waited to present herself until Jim finished taking an order for wedding invitations. "Hello," she said, "I was in here the other day and you Xeroxed posters about my lost dog. I wanted to tell you he's back and to thank you for your kindness." Duncan panted at her ankles.

Jim looked confused for a moment then said, "Oh yeah, the dog with the ribbon. That's nice, ma'am. I'm glad for you."

"He's here," said Lillian and she picked Duncan up to be introduced. The dog blinked in the flashes leaking from the copiers.

Jim looked a little uneasy. "I'm happy for you, ma'am," he said and glanced past Lillian, who turned to see a line of customers lumping up behind her.

"I'm so sorry. I just wanted to say thank you."

"You're welcome," said Jim. "Thanks for using Top Copy."

Driving home, Lillian remembered Jim's cat had just died. "How could I have been so thoughtless?" she asked Duncan and recalled the essential pleasure of the company of dogs: mute tolerance for all ramblings. She sank her right hand in the fur below his collar, steering with the other through thickening traffic to the house. "I'm sorry, Jim," she said. Duncan moaned. At a stoplight, she dipped her finger in the cream cheese and gave it to the dog to lick.

Lillian and Duncan entered the house in near dark. She filled his bowls and nudged him his favorite bone. "We're home, dear," she said. Duncan lapped some water and trundled from room to room, nose twitching at sofas, door frames, potted plants. "What are you looking for, boy?" she asked, walking behind him and switching on lights. "What is it?" she asked. She hooked her thumbs in his armpits and lifted him. Fat and fur rumpled around his neck, front paws paddled the air. He panted. "Where have you been?"

Duncan panted louder. "Who took you?" He started to squirm. "Why did you go with them?" She shifted him into her arms and buried her face into his ears. Not a trace of someone else's perfume, strange food, an unfamiliar city. He must have spent a long time in a car, staring at a blur of New York, Ohio, Kansas. "Why did you go?" she asked him again, taking his snout in her hand. "Were you trying to come home?" He screwed up his eyes and sneezed. She put him back on the floor. In the kitchen, he circled his blanket three times and settled in to twitchy sleep.

She'd never know. How strange it was not to have any idea what Duncan had seen and done, listened to or eaten. Lillian found herself near tears and wondered why. Her dog was home. Her husband still her husband. Her boys alive and thriving. It was that woman in the alley again. The strangeness of not knowing why she'd died, why it wasn't someone else, a neighbor, an old man, a Serb general. You made her up, Lillian told herself. You made her up.

Sitting there in the kitchen filled with blue light, Lillian noticed the blink of the answering machine. Owen had rewired it and now they could receive the messages of the world. There they were. The inaugural calls. Lillian hesitated before pushing the button and was almost relieved that the first one was just a breath and a click. A captured hesitation. No news at all.

To her surprise, the second call came from Claudia Merchant. Lillian and Owen had always laughed at Claudia's molded hair, Bob's signet ring, their trips to exotic places that never seemed to change them. She was taken aback at how it pleased her to hear the thin voice. "Lillian," Claudia said, "I'm astonished you and Owen have one of these things. Anyway, I wanted to ask you a favor about my Siberian iris. I left the corms in the garden and was wondering if you'd mind asking the new family about digging them up." She left her new number as if she'd never had another her whole life and said she'd call later.

"How typical," Lillian said to Duncan, who flicked an ear. Behaving as if she could make a sort of Xerox of her garden. That was Claudia's problem, trying to manage every last detail. No wonder she had a daughter so troubled she lived like a stunned animal in the corner of a hospital room. Claudia, too, had spent her time away, returning glassy in the eye and far too lean.

That's what could happen when you pretended too well that pruned shrubs and smooth hair led to control. Then again, it occurred to Lillian, maybe Claudia knew all that. Maybe she had realized it was a matter of geography and blessed history that bombs hadn't fallen here yet and that given some small shifts and bad decisions, it was just a matter of time. Maybe the South with its shield of magnolias and heat seemed safer. In Sarajevo, Lillian thought, people probably didn't waste time thinking about control or the loss of it. You didn't have time. You had soap to buy, and carrots.

Lillian said, "Wake up, Duncan," and the dog groaned and rolled to expose his belly to the ceiling. In the garage, she picked up a trowel and went to the driveway to wait for Owen. It came to her then why she was disappointed when she heard Duncan was alive and coming home. She'd done nothing to earn all this rich luck. She'd expected at last to be punished.

Owen drove in and the garage light sprang on automatically. Lillian saw her husband bend to gather his briefcase and the rumpled paper. He wore a gray suit, a color some men at sixty could nearly turn to silver, buffed as a trophy. "Hi," said Lillian.

"Is he back?" Owen said. "What are you doing with a trowel?"

"Yes, he's back. Fast asleep in the kitchen as if nothing had ever happened. It's sort of odd." Lillian looked at Owen, the same clear, rare look she gave Duncan at the airport, as if she hadn't seen her husband for weeks. "Claudia called and wants her iris. I felt like digging. Why don't you come?"

"Iris? Now?" said Owen, shifting his briefcase to the other hand.

"Yes, now," Lillian said.

"You're going to march into their garden and start demolishing flower beds? Aren't there twelve children and a stable of au pairs?"

"Probably all at home, too," said Lillian and started walking toward the Merchants' old house.

Owen followed, arguing. "Lillian, it's trespassing."

"I know, Owen," Lillian sighed, holding the gate for her husband. Lights shone upstairs. Children's voices warbled from the windows along with shrieks and splashing water. Bath time.

Owen whispered, "Don't be crazy."

"Are you coming?" she said in a normal voice.

Owen came behind her, treading carefully. The iris beds sat near a new swing set made of hollow metal tubes. Lillian sank to her knees. The earth was warm on top, wriggling and cool with pine needles an inch lower. There was the first one: the corm

Claudia wanted, cool and flaking. "Lillian," Owen hissed behind her. Then she heard a crash. She turned to see he'd slipped on a plastic dump truck and fallen on the swing set, smashing his knee against the seesaw.

"Goddamn it!" he shouted. A light flicked on downstairs. Lillian heard footsteps on hardwood floors. "What did I do to deserve you?" Owen yelled. His briefcase had burst open, page after page of legal paper scattering around the toys.

Leaving the iris and the trowel on the ground, Lillian heaved herself up and went to her husband. She gave him her hand. When he was upright, she dusted his lapels. "We're going to be caught," she said. Her knees were stained with dirt; her hair was probably a mess.

A bulb on the porch snapped on. A tall man in a suit stood there, his face crumpled in a scowl as he peered into the dusk. "What's going on here? Who's there?" he called out.

They stood in the garden, blinking slightly. "Hi," Lillian said. "My name's Lillian. This is Owen. We're your neighbors." She felt blurred and fragile, as if she might not stay whole if she didn't hold hard to her husband. With the other hand, she waved at the angry man, in a gesture that was half surrender, half hello.

a private state

I SAT ON OUR PORCH AND PLAYED WITH THE PLASTIC FINGERS of the skeleton my father had bought in New Orleans during his residency. His name was Louis, in honor of the state, and he'd recently lost another metatarsal. Our moves had not been easy on him. Here in Maine, his elbows rattled in a wind that smelled of salt and stranded crabs. It was Tuesday night, three days before the end of school, and I found myself reciting the names of the bones he still had left instead of solving the last equations of the year.

I was also thinking about Jake Loiseau, the dark boy who sat a row ahead in math. Like me, he was at sea in numbers. The son of the chemistry teacher, it was odd he had no flair for the quantitative. Instead, he had stillness, and I knew it came from living in the same town his entire life. Jake seemed to me to be the essence of Maine, which appeared to be a very private state.

Unlike Florida, our last home, a place I remembered like a short, violent dream, in fragments of alarming colors. The Doctor had only worked there six months when Naomi, my mother, started wondering, often and aloud, if a woman could actually die from humidity. If the Doctor heard the word one more time, I thought he might kick cracks in the pots of bougainvillea, Pensacola's one boon. So last August, he'd called in a favor and found a job at St. Dympna's, a hospital inland from Biddeford. "Spruce, it's got spruce," he said during one of our last Florida suppers, and attacked his dinner in that silver-knife way he had, the style that survived all our dislocations.

Though I was fourteen, no one mentioned schools. But if either of my parents had asked, I could have told them how I handled a new town. You had to touch a place to know it. The cracked paint of a window sash, the wet pole of a parking meter. And as usual, no one was around to talk to. The Doctor was on duty at the E.R.; Naomi'd scrawled a message that said "Out 'til 10." Naomi was vague on numbers, too: 10 might stretch to 11, though she'd dash back before the end of the Doctor's shift. I let the porch door slam and drifted away from word problems. I was starting to wonder what it'd be like to touch not a mailbox flag or the knob on a cigarette machine, but an actual boy. Not that this would happen soon. I was heads taller than the ones I knew, which we all found quite scary.

Heading downtown, I let my knuckles brush hedges that hid noisy families in yards. People had touched each other in those houses and as a result, babies had been born. Toys in colors worthy of Florida crowded their drives. Everyone on our street was home tonight: the Nasons, the Ballards, the Marcottes, names I turned over in my head like smooth stones found on beaches. Next came Mr. Fleming, the butcher, who'd been glimpsed in a woman's slip when his blind was three inches from the sill. All people had seen was a lacy hem and an inch of Mr. Fleming's pale, haired thigh and that was it. Now it was impossible to buy steak without looking twice at his stumpy fingers.

I'd heard about it in the Purity Supreme, in line behind Mrs. Nason who was telling the cashier, the sort of news that made me feel at home somewhere. But passing Mr. Fleming's, I told him silently I'd remember him more for his clean store and honest scale.

Naomi said she'd always had doubts about the butcher. He fit in too well. No matter where we lived, being taken for a native was one of Naomi's great worries. These days, she muttered about chapped, terse northerners and tried to set herself apart with foamy scarves. A boost to her blondness hadn't hurt, either. On Sunday, we'd performed the season's first tinting, an afternoon of busy quiet, slicing lemon after lemon, squeezing out the straw-colored meat on the cone of the juicer.

I wet my head at the tap and waited for the juice to find the slightest scratch. It coursed, thicker than seawater around ears, along the nape. My eyes smarted and ran and salt mixed with sour in the corners of my mouth. It never worked. My hair, the color of tea, insisted on its plainness, but Naomi got all kinds of silky highlights.

With our scalps on fire in a watery way, we wrapped our heads in towels and leafed through catalogs. Naomi admired a wicker birdcage. I showed her a gadget of steel that hid a fistful of tools useful in disasters. If we hadn't just doused ourselves in lemon, our splits in taste might have spoiled the mood. But the catalogs, the cool room, the turban slipping from my pulpy head—the whole thing edged us as close as we ever got to calm. Shivering for beauty in the presence of my odd and pretty mother, I felt for a few moments as delicately modeled as the handle of a bone-china pitcher.

Part of the spell was silence, but on Sunday Naomi put down Nordstrom's summer circular, looked at me and said, "I'm thinking about cutting it all off."

"What?" I said, "Your hair?" I didn't believe her. Naomi without long hair would be like the Venus de Milo with arms. Wrong.

"It weighs me down," she said. I waited, very cautious. Mostly, *this* was how I saw Naomi: slinging forks and spoons in separate slots, shifting lanes on highways. She never paused to confide. Then she went back to Nordstrom's and we slipped into our usual state of not being at all sure where the other person stood.

This was why it helped to touch things like trees and fences, which usually stayed where they were put. I realized then I'd wandered past downtown. My hand was curled around the signpole that marked Sheepscot Street, home of the Dusseaults, an older couple from Québec. We'd spoken a few times, though our shaky holds on one another's language often kept us in the realm of mime. Mr. Dusseault's passion was splitting logs. Un, deux, trois, I heard tonight. He counted when he cut. Madame's linens snapped on the line. Where was she? It being Tuesday, probably Lewiston, visiting her sister, a habit I'd learned about on my last visit.

Then a bug zapper flared next door and I knew the real reason my feet had taken me here. Jake and his father lived one house down from the Dusseaults. My fingers wound into a yew bush, I looked for signs that they were home. But the house looked empty. Jake was pulled to other places, too, if I understood his landscapes in the margins of the math book, all thatched huts and men playing minute guitars. I could have told him to give his palms less bounce. If he'd been curious, we could even have talked about our year in L.A., where we'd lived close to a weak spot in the earth's crust. But there was never an opening, and I was much better at imagined conversations than actual ones. I wasn't even sure he knew my name.

I was about to turn back when I heard laughter on the screened porch. It was a porch like ours but larger, with a sofa and a radio playing jazz, scratchy after coming from somewhere further south. After a moment, I recognized Mr. Loiseau. His voice was so relaxed it took a second to connect it to a man who had to prevent the reckless use of Bunsen burners. Then it struck me that I knew the other voice as well, also at a pitch I didn't often hear. In the zapper's flash, I saw Mr. Loiseau's hands were twined into a woman's. I'd heard the voice. It had to be Naomi, but she was letting someone touch her.

Mr. Dusseault's ax rang, and apart from the thud of metal on wood all my mind could hold was a picture of the Doctor calling for her as he drained a beer can hollow. I was stumbling into the street when a scream went up. Mr. Dusseault was darting around his yard. He raced to his wife's laundry line and grabbed with one hand at a towel. He was moaning now and I saw the flush of blood on the white cloth. "Mother of God," I heard Naomi say. "He's chopped off part of his hand." She stood up, leaving Mr. Loiseau to stare while Mr. Dusseault tore back to his logs, scrabbling on the ground.

"The poor bastard's looking for it," said Mr. Loiseau. That was when they both saw me. The next thing I remembered I was in Naomi's car holding a towel stuffed with ice and what was left of a thumb, still speckled with pine needles. Naomi told Mr. Dusseault to shut up or else he'd make the bleeding worse. I don't think he understood because he yelled "Ma sainte mère" the whole way to the hospital. I sat in the back, a stream of cold sliding down my thigh, too thin to be anything but melting ice.

Inside St. Dympna's, I saw that spots of red had spattered Naomi's shirt, buttoned askew. Then my father rushed into the waiting room. "Naomi?" he said. As a student he'd burned up yards on playing fields, football curled to his ribs, dodging from men the shape of sides of beef. We watched his old movies sometimes and he'd shake his head, smiling slightly. Tonight, hurtling toward my mother, he looked unnerved and tired. I ran to him and pushed the bundle of Mr. Dusseault's finger into his hands. He cradled it to his chest, as if it were a precious, broken toy.

All kinds of people came blinking into the E.R., bent into their particular hurts. I tried to coil myself into the plastic chair, but I'd grown too tall. Then I saw my parents. "Let's go," my father said. In the car, Naomi didn't bother with the seat belt, but the Doctor didn't seem to notice. "Couldn't save the finger," he said to the windshield. "A bad cut." Then silence fell, that terrible kind, where nothing is said but everything that's thought moves sharp and fast. I couldn't have spoken anyway. I felt like I'd swallowed a pot of paste, as if, inside my throat, all the words had hardened to a clear and solid plug.

They waited 'til I'd shut my door for the night. From my bed, I heard shouts shatter in the kitchen. "Tell her to leave," I thought to my pillow, my voice still glued inside my body. I kept imagining her with Mr. Loiseau and was glad my father hadn't heard the curl of their voices, the pleasure.

"I'll do anything you want," he yelled. "What do you want, Naomi?"

"I don't know," she yelled back.

Smelling yew bush on my fingers, I imagined our house on fire, my parents beating at hot panes of glass. Scared at how clearly I could see this, I went to take a shower and made it as icy as I could stand it. Through the sheets of cold, I could still hear them.

The next morning, I walked gingerly through the house as if I were frightened of dislodging something. At school, it was nearly a relief to stare at an old map of the Soviet Union still whole. Science didn't meet today; I could cut math. Then in the midst of the year's last French test, things started to fall apart. Slapping at one of my first black flies, I realized I almost liked Maine. I liked the smell of pine and on windy days, ocean. I liked the drafty house and the row of spruce that lined the fence. I liked knowing Madame went to Lewiston on Tuesdays. It could have been home. In every blank, I wrote in large clear letters "merde."

In history, where we'd just emerged from Gettysburg, I thought that if we stayed, I might acquire an accent. Looking at my classmates, I thought I might acquire friends. I might have had conversations that went beyond "Mr. Feiken is such a dork" or "cool shoes." We listened to Mr. Lincoln's speech. So little, such an echo. I decided to go further. Not a single word at all. Nothing until they agreed to stay.

I'd never spoken much; it got you so involved. I was already tall and didn't need to draw more notice to myself. My thoughts were loud, but when I spoke, the noise seemed like a small rip in the silence. Not talking would mean sealing the quiet off, keeping it whole. Thinking of Jake and how much grace he could capture merely flipping to the next chapter in math, I decided to go further, to do without writing.

I left school early and went to the Purity Supreme, where the only lemons for sale were the sort Naomi never chose for tintings, lesser creatures, small and tough. I bought nine, the number of states that at one time or another we'd called home.

They were sitting at the kitchen table. The Doctor said, "Chloe," like he was surprised to see me. As if I'd been dropped fully formed into his life, instead of having been there all along, his child from the start. Naomi was peering at her fingers and seemed amazed they were still whole.

I put my sack of bad lemons on the counter and pulled out the cutting board. Slicing the first one into quarters, my hand shook. I took a wedge in each fist. Naomi still stared at her fingers. I put a lemon between my lips and bit hard. Pure acid washed my gums, my mouth pouched with a pool of spit. I swallowed, slick seeds and all. A shiver sang down my neck and spine. I slid another wedge between my teeth.

"What are you doing?" my father said. Naomi finally glanced up. I finished the first lemon and carved the next in fours. "What's going on?" the Doctor said.

"Stop it, Chlo," said Naomi. "Stop it, honey," she said.

But I had eight more to go. Chalky roughness coated my teeth, and I was getting used to the sour spray, the shiver of the cloudy acid. I felt cleaner than soap had ever made me, clean from inside. I couldn't stop. Juice sank into papercuts. My eyes streamed. I took bite after bite, cut lemon after lemon until thirty-six quarters lay like cramped yellow smiles on the red counter.

My parents just stared at me until Naomi finally said, "I'm sorry, baby," and went upstairs. Two days later, she was gone. No one noticed I wasn't talking. There wasn't much to say when you saw your father wrap your mother's pearls in chamois cloth. Or twitch a hair from her collar just to have a chance to touch her.

She was going to her mother in Omaha. Before, Naomi said "Nebraska" like she'd escaped from a prison but not without a cost. Now it was the only safe place. She pressed against me a few seconds, chin sharp on my collarbone. I was taller now and she had to reach to stroke my hair.

"Naomi's got some things to work out," the Doctor said as we watched her plane take off. He clapped me on the back so hard I nearly choked. He didn't notice 'til that night I wasn't speaking. "What's wrong here?" he asked when I refused to discuss my bad grade in French. We were at dinner, picking at omelets. I didn't think my body could say everything quite yet, so I wrote on a prescription pad that I wouldn't speak until he said we wouldn't leave here. I couldn't move again, and I underlined "move" twice. He started to cry. I couldn't eat eggs for a long time after that. At the sight of one, even whole and brown, I'd remember the jiggle of the salt shaker as his crying shook the table.

A week before Independence Day, the Loiseaus took off. I overheard Mrs. Marcotte say they were out West, as if it were a slightly criminal destination. Leaving Maine was suspect. When Naomi'd flown away, we'd found sacks of beans and carrots at our door, though neither of us ate a lot that summer.

The Doctor was too busy mending careless tourists. When he realized I really wouldn't tell him what I'd done all day, he'd grab Louis to show me which bones he'd helped to save that shift. Once he went inside to shower, I'd settle back inside of being quiet.

At night, I lay in bed and listened to the spirals of sound the crickets made. To the crunch of my father's feet on the gravel when he came home late and the suck of rubber on the icebox door as he opened it in search of beer. I'd keep an ear tuned to my body's own invisible flow and listen to my bones click longer.

I also nursed a superstition: if I ended my silence, Naomi would come back too soon and it would all start over. It was good to have a break. For once, the Doctor wasn't looking for a job and I appreciated my stillness, though I knew that when Naomi returned, she'd whirl through the house, banishing all signs that time had passed and we had settled. She'd start angling for a fresh start, scared, it seemed, of turning into a woman who just stayed and aged in one place. But for now, the house was ours. Even so, all the way from Omaha, I felt her watching as I made small moves to hunker in.

Despite the Doctor, we didn't own a first-aid kit. I went to town with a long list, but got distracted in the pharmacy by the loops of fake hair stapled to boxes on the shampoo shelves. Mocha and ginger, cinnamon and midnight. Tintings weren't dyes, Naomi insisted, they were enhancements. She called hair coloring shatteringly tacky. But what they were was gorgeous.

Then I spotted Mr. Dusseault in the aisle whose sign said Seasonal Values. I hadn't seen him since the amputation and tried to duck behind conditioners, but I was too tall. He raised his bad hand and ambled to my section. "Bonjour," he said, then pointed to a box labeled "Everyone Loves Scarlet." I lifted it high, waggled it in the air and dropped it in my basket. Silence made my gestures bigger, but Mr. Dusseault didn't notice. This was mostly how we spoke anyway. He smiled and invited me to visit.

I could tell he felt Naomi and I had rescued him. We were simply there, I could have said, and not in savory circumstances, but he knew that, and still he wanted me to come. It was a bond, I allowed, holding someone's severed finger.

Over milky tea, I learned he and Madam were from a village in the far north of the province. They showed me on a map. Their French rushed like cold water over big stones. We played rummy on a scarred table under a tree and Monsieur won, which he enjoyed. They didn't seem to care I didn't say a word.

Some of my happiest times had been with neighbors who didn't speak much English. In Louisiana, Mrs. Vong fed me soups of clear noodles. Señora Lopez in L.A. braided my hair. Sometimes I'd help them iron, make dinner in kitchens that smelled of continents I'd never seen or leaf through photo albums while they explained in Lao or Spanish who these people were. I'd nod as if I understood, which in a way, I did. Those afternoons, I thought I knew what home felt like, and it was a difficult place where you felt complete and full of longing all at once. It was only when I waved good night to the Dusseaults that I remembered to look through the hedge. The Loiseaus were still away.

That night, I colored my hair "Everyone Loves Scarlet." The dye stung more than lemons and sheathed the sink in transparent, exciting maroon. It looked awful. I ruined one of Naomi's monogrammed towels. My father said, "Good Christ." Madame said, "Très joli," but she was just being kind.

People could get used to change. Mr. Dusseault was casual with the hand that had the big raw scar. He even chopped wood, though much more slowly. I helped him pile logs and was getting sleepy and calm in the sun when I noticed a flash of light on metal. The Loiseaus' car was back. Jake sat on the porch, staring at something far away.

All night, I lay inside the quiet and thought about sitting next to him on that sofa, his legs grazing mine. His big-knuckled hand in my palm. I didn't think he'd spoken much that summer, either. But all I'd have to do was call "Jake" through the hedge and he'd look straight at me. He wouldn't be able to help himself. Names were like that. They tugged you into the world. August was going to have a different color.

Temperatures worthy of Florida accompanied the new month. People from Maine faded as thoroughly as lettuce, but the Doctor and I had learned a southern technique. Washcloths and towels chilled in a bowl of water in the fridge, ready to be draped on the body's areas most sensitive to cold. Naomi, who still hadn't phoned, would have hated this heat, but I'd heard it was even worse in Omaha. A filmy scarf of moths rasped against the screen.

The Doctor and I lay on chaise longues in our bandages. Rolling his beer can across his forehead, he said, "Got a call from your mom today." I sat up and a line of water from my neck cloth twisted its way down my back. He never called Naomi "Mom." "She's going to spend the fall out there. Pulling things together." He took a sip of beer. At first, he'd crammed the places I was meant to talk with too many words to describe a simple event. Now, after a month, he seemed to finger the space my answer would have filled, trying to test its exact shape. "Chloe?"

My body cast a block over Louis's bony shadow. "Naomi won't be coming home," the Doctor said. "We've got to pack her stuff and send it out." I stood, picked up a wet cloth and threw it so hard against the screen the moth scarf sprang into the night. I felt a wave in my chest that would have been, if I hadn't stopped talking, a yell that said, "She's supposed to come back." All we needed was a rest. My father watched me, and it was hard to believe he'd ever helped anyone win anything his whole life, much less made a broken bone lie straight. I sat back down and passed him a fresh towel. "Thank you, baby," he said and mopped his face. The screen quit trembling and the moths were floating back when I snapped off the light.

There was no just packing Naomi up. You could box her knives, blouses, and handbags and still she was there, her habits fluttering through my day. The fog of her chamomile facials. The Billie Holliday she played on Sundays. "Just leave," I shouted at her in my head. I applied another layer of "Everyone Loves Scarlet." I tore up hankies that I knew she'd miss.

It was a Saturday of tall, thick heat. The last packages stood on the porch. The Doctor was the color of ash at the bottom of a barbecue. I had to decide something then. I picked up the marker he'd used to write our return address and jotted, "Want to go to the beach?" The pen felt strange in my hand, though I liked drawing the question mark. "Sure," he said, "sure, hon" and I could tell it helped him to act like a normal family faced with a sunny weekend.

The sand was jammed, with Québecois and Mainers spread far as the tide allowed. The Doctor had gathered the energy to find trunks and a pair of flipflops I remembered from Pensacola, but once settled on the beach, he didn't shift from the umbrella. He lay there, staring at its plastic ribs. Naomi had bought it from a catalog. At the time, we'd lived nowhere near a coast.

That was enough to send me straight to the ocean where I let the cold smack the breath from me. If my heels and hands didn't dip below the top layer, I could nearly pretend to be warm. Salt spiked my hair into orange tentacles that Naomi would have been ashamed of. But she wasn't here anymore. She wasn't going to see this evolution of my style, which was both satisfying and not OK. Out here, however, I could handle it. It was all this good northern cold and big salt, shifting and rocking all around me, an atmosphere of sudden change. Then I felt the water roll below my body, looked up and saw a steep moving curve of wave. And then I was, abruptly, inside it.

The next thing I knew I was on my back and staring at the high blue curve of the sky. I thought I knew how those crabs thrown past the high-tide line might feel. Shocked and wasted. Every inch of my body pearled with sand. I sat up and seawater streamed from my mouth and nose. A stripe of kelp plastered my arm.

Fathers went on playing with children. A girl toddled past me with a green bucket and shovel in her hands. I was too old to be missed. The Doctor was probably still staring at the expensive umbrella. But I'd nearly drowned, I wanted to shout to someone. My heart beat unevenly. My breathing hadn't righted itself.

A blue flash of shorts danced past and I saw Jake, a box greasy with fries and hot dogs in his hands. He saw me and slowed on the way back to his friends. There were too many fries for one person.

He had come with actual friends. I wanted nothing more than to crawl inside a shell and seal me and my ugly hair in. I could nearly see why Naomi had to go. When you were a wreck, it took courage to stay visible. "You OK?" Jake asked. I nodded. He crouched down. His shoulders were burned. He had beautiful knees. "Your cheek," he said, "is bleeding."

In the sand, I wrote "I'M OK." He didn't seem to think it strange not to answer aloud. He just read my note in the beach. "You sure?" I nodded again, and he walked back to his friends. But he was by himself. It was just that he was thin and hungry.

I picked my way back to the Doctor. It rattled him, the sand, the cuts, something else I couldn't see. Maybe he'd hoped I was too big to get hurt anymore. Maybe he didn't like it that he still had to watch for me. I cried then, shaking, nearly soundless, the way I cried when I was lost on a beach in a state I didn't remember and for once they'd both been worried sick. "Honey," he said, over and over, fingers dusting the sand from my back, as if I were something he could break if he weren't careful.

My father said he was sorry he had to go to the hospital and I believed him. He'd cleaned my scrapes, made me tuna sandwiches, and kissed my rough hair. There was an experimental lightness to his walk. The moths were late. I wondered if it was because we'd sent the last boxes. I wondered if it was because I'd been deeply tumbled in the North Atlantic.

Then I heard the gate creak and saw Jake and his long shadow standing there. I hadn't realized he knew where we lived, but that was how towns were. If you stayed long enough, people did know things, for better or for worse. "Can I come in?" he said. He waited 'til I waved to open the door. "You're not talking, right? That's what Mr. Dusseault said." I nodded and coughed, ocean still in my lungs. His hair was wet. A part sang down his scalp. At least we were both clean this time.

"You got wrecked out there," he said. I shrugged, but I wanted to say, "Not *wrecked;* just a little roughed up." I hadn't broken any bones or knocked out teeth, had I? I was still whole, wasn't I? Besides, it wasn't personal. Oceans were just that way.

Jake wandered up to Louis and gently touched his ribs. "This is weird, your skeleton on the porch." I pointed to a chair across from me. He sat down and said, "He's missing some metatarsals." I offered him my iced tea. He sipped it. "That's good," he said and that was all for a bit. We sat there, listening to mosquitoes, cats, and sprinklers. He was easy with quiet; it had a curvy softness to it when he was around. It was better than words and so I was surprised when he asked, just as it was getting dark, "You go to the beach a lot this summer?" I shook my head. "Me neither; we were out West the whole time. My Dad and I spent a week in the Grand Canyon. You've got to move carefully in there."

I had already broken my vow. Still it surprised me how nice it felt to take that black marker and print "Why?" in block letters. I could have written all night; there were rolls of paper and jars of pens left over from wrapping Naomi's stuff. I slid my note to Jake.

"Why," he read. "Because it's so big that even little sounds pop these big echoes. It was great but I was glad we were coming back." He looked away then, a little shy. Even when a place was home it wasn't simple. Things were always shifting.

I had questions, I realized. Did his father know Naomi was in Omaha? Then it struck me I didn't know what had happened to Jake's mother. Where was she? I was tired all over. I wasn't ready for this. One word, one thought led to another and then another, a long thick wave of them you had to ride.

Then Jake said, more to the twilight than to me, "I've been wondering something. What happened to Mr. Dusseault's thumb? Where'd they put it?" I hadn't thought about that. I wrote another scrap, "Ask him?"

Jake leaned close to read this next note. "How could you ask someone something like that?" Monsieur, I wanted to say, could stand strange questions. In fact, it would be good to ask him. He'd lost a critical piece, but it hadn't made him run.

The wind was blowing harder now. Louis clanked on his metal pole. He was going to drop a pin in his knee quite soon. Even the springs spanning the plates of his skull were starting to stretch. "Chloe?" Jake said. Hearing him say my name shook me as happily as if he'd touched me. "You know what the bones are called?" I nodded. So he was serious about this becoming conversation and in a rush as quick as the wave, I wanted Naomi there to tell me what to do. But Naomi wasn't very good with men and all their complications, either. Maybe no one was. Maybe that was part of it: you had to find the words that linked you to this new piece of life alone.

Jake held the length of the shin and said, "This one's a tibia, right?" Tapping at the thigh, he said, "And this is the femur?" And he worked slowly up the body, through the pelvic ring, the arms and ribs. I nodded each time. His fingers rested on the clavicle. We were close enough that even in the dark I could see that his nails were bitten to the quick.

Then he pulled me to my feet, fingers on my elbows, careful with me. We were the same height and as bony as the other. He'd grown over the summer and hadn't settled into his new inches yet. It would hurt if our bodies touched. My skin was scraped, his was peeling. "What's this one?" Jake asked and tapped the fragile plastic sternum, the spear-shaped plate my father said protected only one-third of the heart. The rest was exposed. There was only so much a skeleton could do. "Chloe," Jake said. "What's it called?" He tapped again.

"Sternum," I said, because breastbone, more familiar, was so naked for a first word.

safe as houses

THE BATHROOM WALLS WERE FINALLY CLEAN, EXCEPT FOR THE rusty cloud a leak had left behind. Elizabeth sat on the edge of the tub, took a bare foot in her hand and rubbed the arch. It was speckled with chips of purple enamel, paint that most likely came from the family who'd drawn the Pegasus in the attic one dreamy evening in the '60s. Damp curls of different wallpapers lay on the floor. One family had picked midget cardinals in profile. Another chose slashes of bamboo shading silver pagodas.

A year ago, Elizabeth, Andrew, and their daughter, Kate, had moved to this white house at a calm remove from New York. She was still unearthing traces of old occupants: a dog toy in the basement, mittens behind radiators. There were other, more alluring clues. A wedding album with missing pages, the groom in hornrims, the bride with pale, marcelled hair. A pair of kidskin gloves, the leather nibbled.

Her own family's things had slowly rooted in place. Andrew's clematis. Kate's dollhouse which held a plastic boy named Spot and his shelter for homeless cats. You lifted sofa cushions these days and found pencils and dimes. Elizabeth was starting to feel safe here. Her toes sank into the blue fuzz of the bathmat.

If Andrew had been in charge of this job, he would have slapped up the paint, then opened the window to let the breeze clear out the smell. He had felt at home with crisp immediacy, but

Elizabeth wanted to know what happened here before her family arrived. She learned the Mercers had divorced after twenty-five years then the Cohens had another baby. A split followed by an increase; one offset the other, she supposed. Elizabeth picked up a shred of paper: blue men sat inside pagodas, fingers tangled in their beards.

"You could have used hot water and vinegar to get the paper off." An old man stood in the doorway. He was small and carried his coat in a dark oblong over his arm. His pants had perfect hems.

"Who are you?" Elizabeth said, too surprised to move. How had he gotten in? Where else had he been? She imagined the drawers of her bureau wrenched wide. But he didn't look sturdy enough to wrench drawers. She stood up. With relief, she saw she was taller.

"I'm Joseph Krystowicki. Vera's cousin. I should be on that family tree you're working on downstairs." He sketched the air, mimicking the strokes Elizabeth used to draw her genealogical charts. "Vera told me to say hello. You left the kitchen door open." He shifted his coat to the other arm.

"A cousin of Vera's? Is she all right?" Elizabeth asked. Why hadn't he called out? Or phoned?

"She's fine, she's gone to Miami." He waved his free hand in the air. Elizabeth remembered that Vera had mentioned she was thinking of spending a week in Florida; but Elizabeth knew she hadn't said anything about a cousin. "I'm looking after the house. And she told me to help you with your chart," the man said patiently, as if that were enough to explain. "Let's go downstairs." What was strange to Elizabeth was that it seemed like the only proper thing to do.

The man led Elizabeth to the drafting table in the study where a rectangle of archival paper was thumbtacked smooth. It was a tree she was tracing for Vera Kosovsky, her neighbor and a survivor of a labor camp in Poland. Her tree was difficult, the way they often were for Jewish clients, with no way to avoid the many branches pinched short by the war. Families that should have run to the bottom of the page, run right off it, stopped in the middle, hanging there like black and broken chandeliers. Elizabeth imagined Vera looking at all the gaps and saying, in her decisive way, "Well, we can't change what happened. There is no way around the facts."

The man pointed. "There. That's where I should be: Joseph Krystowicki, Lodz, 1925. Son of Avram and Magda." Elizabeth traced the line from Vera: he was her second cousin, born in the same town. Why had she never talked about him?

Elizabeth looked at her feet. It was hard to assert yourself when you weren't wearing shoes. She said, "Mr. Krystowicki, I don't mean to be rude, but Vera hasn't ever mentioned you." He was a formal man. Despite his intrusion, she would never have called him Joseph. He looked as if he were in slight and constant pain. His knuckles were flat and huge as if they had once been smashed.

"We don't spend a lot of time together. But I wanted a change of scene and she wanted someone in the house while she was gone." He looked at her, calm, measuring. "Vera said you were doing this project for her. She said I should help you. My memory is better than hers, for certain things."

Elizabeth felt slightly dizzy. "Would you like some coffee?" she said.

"Please. With sugar." Joseph dipped his head, looked courtly.

When she returned with steaming cups, Joseph was sitting in a chair at the sunny end of the room. Despite his age, his unclear status as visitor or intruder, he made her feel like a hostess still mastering the etiquette of entertaining. Sugar tongs? Why hadn't she thought to arrange a plate of cookies? At least she'd found her sneakers. Standing there with her tray, she realized she often felt callow around those who had lived through the war. They had stood things she could hardly fathom. He was older than Vera, but had her same dry vigor.

Joseph sniffed his coffee. "This makes me think of Rome, those pigeons and statues." He put his nose to the brim and sniffed again. "I am sorry I surprised you."

"That's all right," Elizabeth said slowly, "I was taken aback. I don't usually leave doors open. I'm careful about it, in fact."

"Quite right," he said. "Vera told me about your Kate." He sipped his coffee and closed his eyes for a moment. His accent was strong, Eastern European.

"When was the last time you saw Vera?" Elizabeth asked.

He opened his eyes. "Two years ago. We bumped into each other in Miami. Before that, not since before the war. Imagine that," he said and closed his eyes again.

Elizabeth wondered if he was asleep. Then she asked, "Mr. Krystowicki, why didn't you knock harder? I would have come downstairs."

His eyes snapped opened. "Because you would never have let me in," he said. "You don't like strangers."

It was true. Friendly once she knew who it was, she let her sympathies grow slowly. She often woke in the middle of the night convinced someone was trying to jimmy a window. An historian, she'd tried to train herself to assess sources just as critically, a skill that kept her attuned to personal detail. She taught two classes at the local college: one on U.S. presidents and the other called "Pursuit of Happiness: The Character of Thomas Jefferson."

Elizabeth's students earned their diplomas in fragments, at night, which made her tolerant when they couldn't turn papers in on time. She understood working in pieces from her experience with genealogy, with its hunt for links and separations, its attempts at the neat articulation of relations, so tactile but evasive.

It always amazed her how branches of information just disappeared. All this was why she asked her visitor, "Mr. Krystowicki, why don't I have your information on the chart?"

It was an early summer morning when he had heard the gunfire, the whine of rusted gates, the echoes of boots on concrete. The ones who were left had known someone would be coming soon, Americans or Russians. But it was bad to hear the sounds of an army again, even a liberating one. He had hoped for Americans; they were supposed to have food. The Nazis and their Poles had poisoned the well and burned the warehouse before retreating, although someone had found a bottle of wine in the officers' mess.

Then the Americans appeared, looking like tall, fat babies, with their long legs, their round cheeks. The first thing that had struck him at the evacuation camp was the smell of trees. All of them had been cut down at the lager. But everything was sharp and strange: the stiff arms of the new shirt, the hiss of jazz from a radio. He was beyond hungry, though all he could manage was a little rice. The tea was hot and bitter.

Instead, he walked. He heard the click of his hips as he tracked circles around tents in the light of a half moon. It was better with the sun down. He picked up speed. The air tingled his stubble. He jumped at a sound in the nearby woods, then realized it was the rattle of wind in leaves, as sharp to him as coins rapping glass. Going back to his tent, he ran into two soldiers with dark faces and bright eyes. He was on his knees. They had hands with callused finger tips that lifted him to his feet. One soldier put his rifle down and said, "It's OK, mister, it's OK."

"So that was the first thing I really knew about America," Joseph said. "Those soldiers. It's not the same place now; the soldiers aren't the same. Even then, just because you'd won didn't mean you were a friend to Jews. But it was enough. It made me say, no more Europe."

Joseph lifted his cup to make sure it hadn't left a ring of mist. "In my camp, there were over two hundred thousand of us, Jews from all over, Gypsies, Jehovah's Witnesses. One hundred and seven were liberated." He made a fist that stayed planted on the arm of the chair.

Sun lit his face, his black eyes. He peered out the window, squinting. "It's three o'clock. What time do you have to pick up your daughter?"

Elizabeth jumped. Kate had been the last thing on her mind. Would he like to come to dinner? Was there anything she could do for him? There was still the chart to discuss.

He stood up and said, "No thank you. I will talk to you later about the chart." He complimented her coffee. She helped him with his coat and waited while he wound a muffler around his neck. They left through the kitchen door, which Elizabeth tried twice before she was satisfied that the lock had held.

Elizabeth nestled herself in a cluster of adults wearing sensible boots with crinkled soles. Au pairs, Tortolans and Finns, whispered to each other in the weak suburban light. The northern girls bore the cold with the stare of Samoyeds. The islanders blew clouds of breath on hands curled in ski gloves borrowed from busy mothers. Mothers who cleaned bathrooms, mothers who never had disturbing encounters with anyone, much less sharp, sad survivors of the Holocaust.

Elizabeth thought she would find comfort in the company of American grown-ups after her conversation with Mr. Krystowicki. Instead, she found herself wanting to tell the story to these young foreigners. They looked kind but tough. She wondered if this was why the children who ran to the au pairs seemed so relieved to see them. Did Kate want an au pair? Did she want someone more seasoned than her stay-at-home mother? Should she send Mr. Krystowicki next time? He even had Old World manners.

Steam poured from Elizabeth's nose in plumes, like the smoke from the nostrils of dragons. It was almost time for Chinese New Year. What was it—monkeys, snakes, rats? Kate would know. Her school took almost every culture's history aggressively in stride.

The children burst from the school and the adults dispersed, each holding the hand of a child in a padded coat. Kate and Elizabeth walked in silence, as Kate did not like to be asked how school was. But today, Elizabeth wanted Kate to ramble, to beg her to race to the end of the block, even to insist on television. Instead, she eventually told Elizabeth about Martin Luther King. Their class was learning parts of his dream speech by heart; they were going to see a movie; but they had decided not to do a play about his life. No one felt that they could play Dr. King.

Elizabeth said she could understand: those were big shoes to fill.

"I think he's still here," Kate said.

"Who?"

"The Reverend Dr. Martin Luther King, Jr." Kate glared at her.

"It would be better if he were still here, but he was shot in 1968." What would have happened if King and Kennedy hadn't been shot? Elizabeth wondered how the list of presidents in her class would have changed. Among other things.

"That doesn't mean anything," said Kate. She tore down the street, knapsack bobbing. With Kate bounding into her own world, Elizabeth felt abandoned. She realized Mr. Krystowicki had said he would help with the chart and then had not. She remembered the afternoon she found out about Dr. King. She was slouched, twelve, ravenous. The refrigerator shelves were empty of almost everything except mustard and relish. No one had been to the store. That was when she heard the television and her mother crying.

The answering machine had taken a message from Andrew, who asked plaintively if she would mind making dinner tonight.

Elizabeth's husband worked with an agency that built housing for the mentally ill. His battles for justice were beset, operatic. Sometimes, however, they ended in concrete results. Houses were put up. People got to live in freshly carpeted homes instead of hospitals. Andrew believed that new carpets were a kind of progress. Elizabeth admired his persistent belief in humans' ability to become better.

At dinner, Andrew was still fuming. A residence for schizophrenics was slated for a tony neighborhood of Brooklyn. Residents were getting edgy. Andrew attacked his spaghetti as if it were one of the nervous homeowners. "Will one of these people go after my children? Will it smell funny? One of them actually said that today."

"There's room in the attic," Kate said. She made herself a green mustache with two beans.

Elizabeth and Andrew looked at her. Andrew said, "Get those beans off your face, Kate. These people need more attention than we can give them. Medication, doctors. Elizabeth, what happened in the bathroom?"

Kate said, "Yeah, there was paper all over the place." She arranged beans on her plate in the shape of a trapezoid, the new shape in math this week.

Elizabeth realized she hadn't told them about Mr. Krystowicki. As she looked at them, Andrew's hand on his wine glass, Kate's fingers glossy with butter, she decided to keep the news to herself. A domestic secret. Like adding cumin to the potatoes although Andrew claimed he didn't like it when in fact he never noticed. "Sorry," Elizabeth said, "I got caught up in other things." It was even pleasant and a little shameful to lie like this and to wrap the day's oddness around herself.

Kate said, "Dr. Martin Luther King would have had sick people in his house." She pushed her chair back from the table.

"Katie, come on back," Andrew said. Kate had Elizabeth's eyes and a hint of Andrew's nose. But she was clearly separate, too, the way Andrew was: angular, away on his causes. Filled with their own news. Elizabeth was sure they withheld sections of their days. On her charts, a short white space lived between two names connected in marriage. In genealogy, you never lost sight of how families were individuals that history and habit, force and affection, had roped together, however tenuously.

That night in bed, Elizabeth lay with hands cradling her head and thought about her first trip with Andrew. Graduate students in the early '80s, poor and ratty, they had decided to go to Prague, on whose edges armies had stopped, whose castle had every Gothic spire intact, where American dollars could be stretched.

Elizabeth had hoped for something languid in Prague. Golden leaves of plane trees floating on the Moldau. But the city that July was wrapped in a thin hot cape of pollution that pitted the facades of buildings in the Stare Mesto. Anytime, she felt she might bump into Kafka, high knobs of color in white cheeks. She jumped whenever someone coughed.

Andrew liked it. He was even excited when he thought a chain-smoking man with sideburns was tailing them. But there were so many men like this that it was impossible to say. The spit that flew with practiced skill at the heels of Russian speakers, the stiff faces of the children: it should have horrified her. Instead, the city made her long for Italy, terra-cotta palazzi, caves of saints. Prague's only redeeming feature was the cheap and excellent beer.

Elizabeth and Andrew were drinking from exaggerated flagons as she told him she wanted to leave. At marble tables, Cuban and Vietnamese workers, employed to restore crumbling theaters made the room sharp with spiky bits of language.

"You should love this, Elizabeth," Andrew told her. "What hasn't happened here?" That was the trouble. It made her uneasy to be in a place with more soldiers than children. Women who stared at you from shops with flat, unflinching eyes. And other things she'd only read about, like Lidice. "Come on," Andrew said.

He took her to a boulevard flanked by stately buildings studded with wrought-iron fruit and reliefs of classical heads. Blinding white, but despite their cleanliness, they looked uneasy, conquerors not quite on the moral side. Elizabeth knew they sat on the foundations of the ghetto, whose only traces were a triangle of cemetery and a synagogue that served as a museum.

It was late afternoon. Inside the gate, the gravestones covered every open space. They came out of the ground at strange angles, like old teeth. Many were cracked in half. Elizabeth tried to trace families from one end of the plot to the other, but most inscriptions were in Hebrew. Some were so old their carvings were less like letters than hollows fingers left in sand. The oldest stone she saw was dated 1383; the newest she could find for a girl named Nazdhevda in 1939. After that the Jews of Prague died elsewhere.

Andrew came up behind her and wrapped his arms around her waist. Although they hadn't known it then, Kate was a slender sprout inside her. Elizabeth had never thought of their child as having come too soon. It was the only thing she had ever been quite so clear about.

She wondered if Mr. Krystowicki had relatives buried in Prague. He had a dustiness that reminded Elizabeth of the city. But then how did he know about Rome? She pressed her body along Andrew's, trying to obliterate all the space between.

Elizabeth spent the next few days waiting for Mr. Krystowicki to come back. When at home, she left the front door unlocked. She painted the bathroom slowly, waiting for a tip on brush technique. The weather had been perfect, melting all snow, so there was no need to ask if she could shovel the walk for him. In the air, there was a smell of false spring.

When she went out, however, she made doubly sure that the alarm was on. She didn't want to come home and find him tilting pictures on their spiraled wire back into place. Or making changes to the chart without asking. Would he do something like this? He had a kind of rough authority that made her wonder.

Maybe this was a trait he shared with Vera. Once Elizabeth had bought bird seed on sale and Vera had come to pick it up. Vera had hoisted the sack and said her abrupt thank you when she saw a pile of jewelry on the counter. "What's that?" she'd said to Elizabeth.

There were marcasite earrings, an opal ring loose in its setting. A small and tarnished pile of baubles, jewelry Elizabeth's grandmother once owned. "I'm taking it to be cleaned."

"Your grandmother's," Vera had said. She shifted the sack to her other hip and picked up the ring. "There was a story in the family that when the pogroms started, my grandmother buried all her gold in an orchard. And later, when the orchard died, there was one tree that always bloomed. Ha." She put the ring down. Then she turned to Elizabeth. "Those charts you do. Would you try to do one for me? I'll write out what I remember, then we can go from there."

Elizabeth had said, "Of course, Vera." When Elizabeth went to open the door, the sack slipped from her neighbor's grasp and split on the kitchen floor. Yellow stubs of corn and sunflower seeds peppered the rag rugs. Vera had laughed and apologized. She helped Elizabeth carry the rugs into the yard and shake the seeds in wild wide arcs. She was still very strong. Elizabeth had seen the twist of muscle on her forearms as she shook the carpets into the wind. Birds arrived in instant, chattering flocks. "Maybe we'll have sunflowers in the spring," Elizabeth said.

"No, those seeds are dead. Besides, the birds will find every last one." Cardinals swooped through the yard for days, round eyes fever bright, then just as suddenly, disappeared.

By the end of the week, Mr. Krystowicki had yet to be seen. Now Elizabeth had almost finished the chart and she wanted to talk to him. But now Kate was behaving strangely. Today her daughter rushed out of school wearing a dragon mask, painted red with staring black eyes. Two streamers of ribbon, sewn with woolly black loops to the dragon's ears, snapped in the wind. Kate wouldn't take it off for dinner. She announced it was the Year of the Fire Mouse.

"In the south, they do dragon dances. In the north, they do lion ones. I'm being southern Chinese with Mee Lin." Her voice was muffled, coming out of the slit she'd left for the mouth.

Andrew was pleased if a little bemused. Elizabeth knew he liked anything that opened the world wide for his daughter. It was part of progress. But would they learn about Tibet and Mao? What about the fact that other cultures were more than masks and dances and cheerful American interpretations of holidays? When was the news about Hitler on the syllabus?

Seeing Kate try to push a pea through the mask mouth made Elizabeth wonder if there weren't plenty of time to tell her about Auschwitz, the Cultural Revolution, and Jim Crow. Kate then told Elizabeth, "Did you know that if you eat a cup of apple seeds it can kill you?" If she was attuned to dangers as domestic as that, she would catch on fast enough.

That night, Kate stormed into Elizabeth and Andrew's bedroom. She stood on the threshold and said loudly, "Dr. Martin Luther King was in the attic."

Elizabeth sat up and said, "Come here, sweetie. How do you know?"

"I saw him standing in front of Pegasus."

"You went up there?"

"He asked if Pegasus could fly."

"What did you tell him?"

"That he was a painting, that he couldn't really fly."

"What did Dr. King say?"

"He was sorry. He must have got the wrong house. And then he left."

Elizabeth knew that Kate wouldn't ask if she could sleep in her parents' bed. She and Andrew had trained her early to spend the night on her own. She was better at it than they were. Elizabeth said, "Hop in, Katie."

Andrew woke up enough to say, "Hi, bird. Your feet are cold." Kate was already asleep.

The next morning, Elizabeth woke up in a tangle of sheets and legs. Kate's hair was in Elizabeth's eyes, one of Andrew's hands was pinned beneath her hip. A warm and awkward mass of bodies. Elizabeth wrapped an arm around Kate's stomach and felt the twitch of a vein in her daughter's chest. Andrew turned over. Kate snuffled. Elizabeth only wanted to stay here in bed, safely, uncomfortably wrapped around each other. Andrew yawned. "Morning," he said to Elizabeth and pulled his hand from under her. "My hand's asleep," he said and shook it. "What was that about last night?"

"A bad dream," said Elizabeth and Kate shifted. Elizabeth's foot poked into the sharp air beyond the blankets.

Elizabeth sat in the bus seat, a folder full of student papers on Lyndon Johnson's suitability as president in her lap. Some of her students were intent on proving his involvement in the Kennedy assassination, but she insisted they work in the escalation of the war as well, so as to widen the range of their obsession. The bus pumped along home, fast for once.

She would have the house to herself tonight. Andrew was at a town meeting on his new project, no doubt feeling besieged. Kate was at Mee Lin's for the night. The friendship had grown since the New Year. Elizabeth would be able to finish Vera's chart. She would sit at her table, surrounded by the bound genealogies, the stacks of Xeroxes, and write out the last names in clear black ink. Her results would be slim but then, she resolved, she would take it over there. She still hadn't seen Mr. Krystowicki. The light had been on each night. The garbage had been put out. One small bag of it, a knot of black plastic sealing it shut. She had called a couple of times but there'd been no answer. Vera didn't own a machine.

As the bus lumbered around potholes, Elizabeth thought about the discussion in her Jefferson class. People were divided about Sally Hemings, Jefferson's slave, supposed mistress, and mother of his children. Mr. Brewster said the morals of the president's era were different and we couldn't condemn Jefferson because he hadn't behaved according to our lights. Mrs. Harpole said it was bad enough that the author of the Declaration of Independence had been a slave owner; it was hard enough to reconcile that, much less children whom he'd never had the guts to acknowledge. The rest of the class aligned itself to one position or the other.

"The evidence isn't compelling either way," Elizabeth had said, which was true but it sounded a bland compromise. Mr. Brewster tucked his pen firmly in his binder. Mrs. Harpole rummaged in her handbag. Everyone was disappointed. The answer didn't have the ring of authority, which was what people always expected from teachers.

"Anyway," Elizabeth said as chairs started to scrape, "Part of this is about having to wrestle it out for ourselves. Even the people we'd like to admire are complicated." How do we weigh things like Dr. King plagiarizing? Kennedy's infidelity? Jacket zippers rasped. Mrs. Harpole said she supposed the children of Nazis loved their parents.

Elizabeth listened to the rush of air as the bus doors opened and closed and, lost in the odd rhythm, nearly missed her stop. In the doorway of the house, she saw Mr. Krystowicki, wearing a hat with furred flaps. The weather had turned cold again. The sidewalks shone with a thin sheet of ice.

"Hello," he said, and took off his hat. Elizabeth stamped the cold mud off her feet and said, "I'm glad to see you, Mr. Krystowicki. I hope you haven't been here long. Would you like coffee?" She realized she was looking forward to the rest of his story.

"Please," he said, dipping his head in a courtly way Elizabeth recognized. Vera did this, too, Elizabeth thought. Was it inherited? Or a reflex of their time and culture? She imagined those small and civil responses were hard to erase, even after the camps. How you held a fork. The nod to greet strangers. Or, she thought, as Joseph folded his scarf into the sleeve, maybe those were exactly the sorts of gestures that had to be learned again. She brought sugar tongs this time, which he used expertly. He even helped himself to a piece of shortbread. Elizabeth settled down across from him.

His papers were processed quickly. He told the agent handling his case he wanted to go to Rome. Apparently it was easier to get American visas in Italy. The man raised a bored eyebrow and said, "Fine. You're a free man." That made him unexpectedly uncertain. Italy. It had seemed like such a good idea. He admired the few Italians he knew. It would be a good place to leave Europe behind. Now he wasn't so sure. Still, he found himself on a train to Rome, with women in headscarves and men as thin as nails. No familiar faces in Rome, but then again there wouldn't have been many in Lodz, either. Once he arrived in Italy, though, his confusion had continued.

He missed speaking Polish. He lived in an apartment with Jews from a handful of other shattered countries. Their common language was German but they would not use it. Instead, they spoke barbarous Italian. Some were trying to learn English. They lived for the occasional newspapers that made their way from Poland, Yugoslavia, Russia, even though the papers were packed with lies and had less news in forty pages than five minutes of the BBC. Maybe, too, he was hoping to see a name of a relative or friend, but in that case, if it showed up, it could only mean misfortune. However, it became something of a mission to find these newspapers. It gave you something to do when work dried up.

Their Sicilian neighbors complained about the smell of cabbage in the stairwell, but at least it covered the stink of rancid oil. He prowled around the Piazza Navona, as bony as the cats that tried to wrap their tails around his shins. He rolled cigarettes with other refugees in the shadow of the plaza's fountain and watched water stream over the long marble bodies. Everyone was hungry. Even cabbage became hard to find.

People kept leaving for America, bundling clothes and dictionaries into cracked leather bags. But he couldn't bring himself to go. He worked a little, here and there. He made some friends. There was the daughter of a grocer in the Trastevere who used to sell him potatoes. Once she'd saved him an orange.

One night in the Via del Corso, a fight broke out. A crowd of drunk Italians closed around him and a few friends as they left a *caffè*. A dancing, angry circle of boys who had had too much wine. He'd seen so much worse it was hard to even be that scared. He had started to recover a little strength. He could slip out under their arms any time. Then one of them said, "Dirty Jew, get out of Italy!" *Sale ebreo!* Over and over. And then he didn't remember much after that except the warm glass of the wine bottle he yanked from the hand of a man with dark curls. The boy whose neck he had slashed with the bottle he'd broken on the curb lay slouched against the grill of a bread truck. He remembered the smell of bad wine. He remembered the blue truck, the word "Pane" in white script, the painting of a long Italian loaf.

His friends ran with him. He bought fake papers. He became someone else. He moved to America as that someone else and eventually became a clerk in a New York bank. He paid back those friends who spent so much for the papers and the ticket. At least he sent money to them; whether they got it or not he had never known. Maybe his dollars gave some girl a new hat and gloves. Most of them were probably dead now. Some were perhaps in Israel. They were not even family.

He sat in the chair, coffee grown cold as before. Elizabeth looked at his old, square hands. It was hard to see them as hands that had slashed the neck of a boy. She could see them lifting the gilt-rimmed pages of ledgers and also, looking at the knuckles, wielding tools. She stood up. Her own hands were ticked with red and black marker, from papers and drafts of charts. "We should finish your tree," he said.

"Vera knows this?" Elizabeth said.

He said, "No. She doesn't want to know."

"Why are you telling me?" she said. "What am I supposed to do?"

He shrugged. "It was time. There's the tree." He pointed.

"But why do you care?" Elizabeth's voice rose. "You or Vera?" Why would either of them invest any importance in anything as flimsy as a piece of paper? Three feet by two feet, which, like all paper, burned above four hundred degrees.

"It's something," he said. "This is America." Was he smiling?

"Go on then," she said, "make the corrections." She thumbtacked a new piece of paper down next to the draft and handed him a black pen. He hunched over the blank piece and made a deft vertical stroke. Working quickly, he built a city of black lines on the page. Then he started writing names. It was Hebrew, with all its unfamiliar serifs. "Wait," said Elizabeth. "I can't read it. Tell me their names. Let me see where I was right." There had to be some small things that were clear.

He pointed his pen at one pair. "Anastasia and Moses Guttman, the great grandparents of my paternal uncle." Elizabeth had found them. Every time he wrote a new name, he translated for her. He smelled like a clean, elderly man. His collar was spotless. She stood next to, even brushed her shoulder against, a man who, nearly fifty years ago, left another for dead in a Roman street.

The names he knew were the old ones. Witoski, Keppelman. She had found many of them, but after the war, the blanks were still blanks. "Nothing there, Mr. Krystowicki? Are you sure? Your family is quite finished?" Suddenly, Elizabeth found herself angry. Angry at the abrupt end of the tree. Angry he had told her as much and as little as he had. Angry at this old, battered man for being so much more complicated than a victim. And most of all, for keeping her from feeling safe.

He walked out to the front hall. "Vera comes home tomorrow."

Where was Andrew? How had she let Kate spend the night away, even once? Elizabeth was wild to see them but asked, "Which name did you write down, Mr. Krystowicki?"

"Good night," he said and let himself out the front door through which Elizabeth saw him framed for a moment by the pair of lindens at the end of the walk, branches ripe with buds, lulled by the warm days into thinking it was time to open.

pacific

HELEN LOOKED OUT AT THE ROUGH WATER AND THOUGHT "Pacific" was not the name she would have chosen for this ocean. There was nothing peaceful about these waves with the profiles of sharks. The horizon swung with the boat. She wondered if the whales distinguished tracts of water the way humans did, had codes in their click-and-whistle language for Atlantic, for Indian, for dangerous reef and leaky tanker. What happened when an engine dulled the message? What if their sonar started to wobble, if the rings of sound became dented, imprecise?

The boat lurched. Helen's ring smacked the metal railing, which reminded her that Sam, who used to scold her when her imagination turned Gothic, wasn't here. She felt better when she remembered he went green at sea and was grateful she had some instinct for the nautical.

It had been two days since this group of whale watchers motored out of San Diego, and they'd only seen a distant flock of seabirds, mute *V*s dipping in the wind. As she stared at the waves, Helen couldn't stop thinking about the barracudas and the mantas like wet black capes gliding underneath. The voices of the newlyweds from Boulder passed, the pages of one of their guide books rattling in the wind. Helen's period was eleven days late. She wondered if sharks nursed.

Helen didn't notice that the birds had moved closer until she heard Melissa, the trip's naturalist, call out, "The willets are visiting!" Helen muttered The Willets Visit, thinking it sounded like the title of a children's book where roguish boys from Cornwall invade the house of Kensington cousins. She wanted to watch the birds, but Melissa's recitation of their feeding habits—dead crab and trash—dulled their novelty. Could using phrases like "migration vector" eventually ruin Botticellian beauty? Melissa's skin was as pink as the curve inside a conch shell.

Several of the passengers gathered around the young woman in the stern of the boat. The newlyweds, Sue and David, hovered next to the Donaldsons, a family from Westchester. The mother was blowzy, but the man was tan, still trim, restless. Their two children had the slippery paleness of subversive adolescents. Dr. Marquand, an older gentleman, folded the corner of a page in his bird book. They were all caught in Melissa's spell of science: she could make the leathery eggs of tortoises seem as commonplace as gravity. In truth, it wasn't quite so dry. The listeners wanted facts and magic. Sue, twisting a bracelet so it pressed an antinausea nerve in her wrist, cocked her head like a willet. Anne, in a kerchief and a sweater that looked like it had used the whole alpaca, peered dreamily out at the waves.

Even though Helen was curious about Melissa's lore, she stayed put. Staring at the laces threaded through her new sneakers, she thought about the rolling hand of the ocean on the iron underside of the *Atlantis* and tried to remember why she'd wanted to spend two weeks of April with her unhappy husband searching out the gray whales. They were, she was sure, royally indifferent to humans bobbing around in a stiff-keeled boat. In spite of all this earnest interest, the animals just steered themselves from Mexico back to the Gulf of Alaska, where no one could follow them, not even Jacques Cousteau with his matchless accent.

In late March, one week after Sam had left, Helen was correcting the proofs of one of Jan Van Oort's pet projects, an encyclopedia of animals featuring plate after shiny plate. Jan ran the small publishing house in Boston where Helen edited children's books. "Ruinous," Jan said, standing behind her. His accent was almost as craggy as Cousteau's, but he was Dutch and liked Boston because its weather was even worse than Amsterdam's. "I am courting bankruptcy with this book," he said, rubbing his hands together. Jan got great pleasure from his unequivocal command of English.

He bent to examine one of Helen's scrawls, that cuneiform of proofreaders, which dotted the margins red. "What's this?" He shook his head. "What kind of drugs are you taking, Helen love?"

He pointed to a section of text on amphibians, where Helen had turned the phrase "the density of water," into "destiny of water." The day before, she'd forgotten to hyphenate the name of a newly married author, one of the four who kept the house out of debt.

"Helen," Jan sighed, "Alexa and I had an idea." Alexa, the copy editor who worked in the next cubicle, came to Helen's desk. "What about taking the trip alone? Screw Sam. Go enjoy yourself," Alexa said. She settled her arms across her chest, something she did when about to offer authors advice to give their writing fiber. Helen had never known her to be tempted to put two *L*s in "pavilion."

"It seems," Helen said, fingering the proofs, "my life is in need of extensive revision." Then she burst into tears and the red corrections bled into the black type. Jan and Alexa had been kind: lots of bone-shattering claps on the back from Jan, an offer from Alexa to keep the cat for two weeks. Then she was there, in the eerie pinkness of San Diego, arriving the day before the *Atlantis* was to leave. What if the boat sank? Should she tell Sam what to do with the cat, the plants, her sweaters? Was he still in Baton Rouge? She sat on a bed which could have fit her and Sam and twelve children.

When Helen fled the hotel, the clerk called, "Off to the Zoo?" But she didn't think she could face families admiring okapis and instead found herself walking down boulevards gray with the nervous shadow of palms. Buena Vista, Alameda, I am lost in a sea of Spanish names, Helen thought. Then the pavement shivered. Coconuts dropped from the trees and rolled, lopsided and hairy, underneath parked cars. An earthquake? People strolling past in macaw-bright shirts wandered just beyond the range of the rustling trees. Although she'd been worried about acquiring sea legs, Helen was glad to be boarding the next day. It was too easy to picture California as a section of graham cracker, ready to snap off at the perforated line and crumble into the milky sea.

But what am I doing in the middle of an ocean with a shipful of strangers, Helen thought, people who felt it was fine to bounce around in a suspect old tuna boat and scout for whales. At least they didn't have harpoons. She turned to face the water, closed her eyes and felt queasy, out of place. She should have been tucked behind her desk staring out at the dome of Boston's State House, a golden egg wrapped in fog. She should have bought a home-pregnancy test and called her mother. She should have been there, not gliding over an ocean where the sun set on the wrong side.

Helen got the sense that something had disturbed the air close by and looked up to see a willet. It dangled near her head, dipping like a mobile. She said, "Hello, bird," and in a way that made her uneasy, it answered. Just behind it, Helen saw something wrinkle the water's surface. Something was stirring there, and then she saw thin spray and the crest of an enormous head. They were really here. They were real. Until now, she hadn't quite believed they were real.

Whale breath misted the air. They were close. The first shot through the surface and Helen saw an enormous gray eye. Sheets of water streaming from its body, the whale rose from the ocean and pivoted on its tail. Front flippers pointing toward the sky, it opened its wide mouth. Baleen flashed. In the animal's brief spiral against the sky, she tried to take in the span of its back scratched with whorls like giant lichen. When it fell, its supple weight slammed the water and only then, on its way back down, did the flukes fan into view. Bubbles glittered for a moment after the whale left, then came a flat and magic stillness, which shimmered there for seconds before the waves erased it.

Everyone clustered at the railing, staring at the stretch of ocean where the whales had played. Seven had surfaced, pushing up from under tons of salty water for what seemed to be the sheer pleasure of entering another element. The sight had struck the passengers dumb. Even Melissa was quiet. Helen unwrapped her hands from the railing and noticed they were stiff. Anne and Sue stood next to her, rubbing blood back into fingers. No one had realized how hard they'd held on. Dr. Marquand was still watching. For a moment, there was calm. No questions, no photos. When talk leaked back—Have you ever seen anything like it? Isn't that what they call spyhopping?—Helen had to go below.

Lying in her wedge-shaped bunk, Helen listened to her heart pound. She had never seen anything play with such abandon. Water sloshed at her porthole and she tried to remember the smell of whale spray, its blend of fish, warm seaweed, and something oddly human. She realized she liked sleeping below the waterline and hoped to wake to a flipper or a tortoise beak tapping against the glass. Mrs. Donaldson had insisted on changing to a higher cabin, but Helen liked to listen to the thrum of the engine, the crew's quiet tinkering.

Right now she was more aware of the newlyweds and the sharp words they were exchanging about who forgot to bring 200-speed film. The southern light was going to stain the silver emulsion black, give them dark rectangles instead of pictures for their first trip as a publicly united pair. Voices rose. Helen hoped their bracelets protected against more than upset stomachs.

Early in her marriage, she hadn't minded scrapes like that with

Sam. She'd write him apologies on deckle-edged paper. He'd kiss the bone of her jaw down to her chin. They hadn't done those things in years. Helen shifted in the bunk and became aware that she couldn't stretch to her full length. Sam would have had to curl up like a comma. If she were six months pregnant, she couldn't have fit in the slit of the shower.

It was a possibility. Helen had been feeling sick, but everyone had, thanks to the combination of diesel fumes and fried food. But she was quite late now. Helen, your husband's just left you, Alexa would have said. You're out of whack. Was that the twitch of a cramp? Her hands traveled to her belly, still its regular size. Children. One of the reasons she and Sam had splurged on this trip. They'd finally acknowledged a long-settled coolness, and in December, Helen found the Pacific sea-life brochure at a travel agent's, crammed with photos of flukes and seals, lovely, slick, and clearly warm-blooded. Helen imagined they would watch whales, turn slightly golden in the western sun, and talk reasonably about babies. As if babies induced reason. As if you could talk about anything but whales once you'd seen them.

Then a week before they were supposed to go, he'd told her he'd taken a leave from the paper. "So the *Globe*'s not big enough for you?" she'd snapped. He wanted, he said, to see the heartland again. "I'll come with you," she yelled when she saw he meant it. But he said no. All she did then was smack the table so hard an empty wine bottle thudded to the ground.

He looked at her and said, "Your hair's a mess. It looks great." They made love then, for the first time in months. He had still gone. Helen's head ached. It was time for dinner. On her way up, she stacked three rolls of the right kind of Kodak by Sue and David's door.

Passengers were assigned to tables and Helen had been lumped with the two others traveling alone. Dr. Marquand, a recent widower with gentle, spacy eyes, settled himself next to her. Anne arrived a minute later. Helen had the bunk next to hers and last night listened to a cough that rolled like a wave through the older woman's lungs. Anne helped repair Mayan pottery in a museum in Philadelphia. They had traded these slight basics last night, while pork chops slid around their plates and the boat pitched in heavy surf.

Tonight, no one touched their food. Everyone spoke in quick voices about the sighting. Hands swam through the air, in imitation of the long backs. Even the Donaldson children sat up straight. Melissa glowed, even as she called the whales "cetaceans."

During the next few days, there was even the possibility of touching the creatures. Passengers would pile into a twenty-foot motor boat—steered by the silent blond crew, the tuna boat's old hands—and lurk at the edges of the breeding grounds, Mexican lagoons another day to the south. Mothers and calves were drawn to the small engines and sometimes got curious enough to come inspect these humming fish on the edge of their bays. Helen was both appalled and riveted by the thought of touching something as large and alive as what she saw today. They moved so quickly. They were so clearly aware.

"Pretty spectacular," Anne said.

"Yes." Helen wasn't sure she was ready to engage in whale banter just yet.

"Is this your first time?" Dr. Marquand asked her.

"Yes, before today, I was innocent of whales." To her surprise, Helen waved her fork in the air.

Anne laughed. It was hard to tell the sound from her cough. "The first time I saw them, I burst into tears when they left. I felt totally abandoned."

Dr. Marquand said, "Perhaps it's because they've gone back to the sea and we can't." Being anchored to land seemed to sadden him. Helen remembered one of Jan's books, a money-maker on ocean fauna. He'd reproduced pictures of whale skeletons: under the pads of skin and fat, the almost useless front flippers were hands, the remainders of how they managed, after an unhappy era as mammals on earth, to crawl back to where they'd come from.

"Isn't that it? Isn't that why they got so big?" the doctor continued. Helen wondered how many nights he had spent lulling himself to sleep with stories of big, warm fish. She imagined him in a single bed, whale book propped over his nose, in his dreams a bearded merman who swept past fans of coral on a dolphin's back. With water to support them, he told the women, there were no limits to how heavy they could get. "But not me," he added. "Negative buoyancy."

Then he said to Anne, "That's a bad cough you've got."

Anne said, smiling, "It'll be the death of me." Helen and Dr. Marquand looked at their plates. Anne said, "I just thought I'd go crazy trying to piece together one more pot and waiting for my hair to grow back. So this was my Christmas present to myself."

Helen took her cue from Dr. Marquand, who nodded and looked calm, professionally detached. He unbuttoned a shirt pocket and showed them a brown vial. "Nitroglycerin," he said frankly, now that one frailty had been revealed. "My doctor told me to have the bypass done last month but April's the best time to see the whales." The crew was coming round to collect the plates, most still full. Other passengers followed Melissa into the main cabin to watch a presentation on endangered pinnapeds. In the morning, they would visit a colony of elephant seals. But Helen wanted to sit here with Dr. Marquand and Anne. She wanted to settle her elbows on the table, sip coffee that sloshed over the lip of a blue cup and avoid the topic of any remotely threatened species.

"Your husband wasn't able to make it?" Dr. Marquand asked.

Helen looked at her ring and was quite suddenly uncertain if she should wear it anymore. "Right now, Sam's just this voice that calls from Baton Rouge once in a while." Her coffee spilled some more. "He'd rather talk about zydeco than whether or not he's coming back to Boston."

Anne sighed and Dr. Marquand said, "Silly man." He ordered them all more coffee, although none of them drank it. They sat in their booth, hands wrapped around the hot, thick mugs.

Helen woke in the middle of the night, not to the tap of a flipper on the porthole, but to some creak in the boat. The air in the cabin felt muggy and she wanted to look at the Pacific by herself. Were the whales back? Melissa had said they were young males heading toward the breeding lagoons. Speeding along, Helen thought, to cash in on the carnal festivities further south. But on deck Helen saw little past the glow the light cast from the captain's cabin. Phosphorous flared as the prow cut through the ocean, but beyond that, there was just a shifting, rushing blackness. A tang of pine scented the air, a land smell carried from the island they would visit tomorrow. A few weak stars through clouds. No Alexa, no Jan, no Sam.

Helen wondered where he was, imagined him leaving Louisiana and wandering in a Kansas wheatfield. She doubted he would make it much past the Mississippi. She doubted he would make it back to Boston and for once this thought didn't leave her feeling like someone had shoved her head in a bucket of cold water and kept it there.

She was just Helen, in her new sneakers with the undone laces and ragged bathrobe. But maybe not. What if there were the beginnings of a baby, rocking like a tethered seahorse in her belly. In the books she corrected, parents were relaxed and resourceful, uncannily attuned to developmental stages. She had no idea if she'd be good at that or not. You couldn't edit children. They came with mistakes and problems wound into them from the start. Then the parents could start adding their own. Even with Sam puzzling through it with her, she wasn't sure she could imagine such complex immersion. Alone, it seemed absurd. Chilled, she started to make her way back to the cabin, but she stumbled on the gangway as the boat lurched against a wave.

She barely felt the hit, though she had an impressive welt on her arm the next morning. At breakfast, Dr. Marquand said, "Oh my, look at that nastiness," and took her elbow.

Helen had hoped the collision might knock the blood from her, but instead said, "It's my Melissa vaccine. Anti-antimystery."

"Oh, really," said Anne, who had added dark glasses for the day's trip to see the seals. "I didn't know they'd found a cure."

"Quite useful," said Dr. Marquand, still examining her arm. "Next time try not to break so many blood vessels."

Melissa cried, "Time to go! Remember, the animals are quite tolerant of the human presence but you should respect their limits. Touch with your perceptions, not your hands."

"Touch with my perceptions, my eye," muttered Dr. Marquand.

"The males," said Mrs. Donaldson. "They won't charge or anything? On the National Geographic special, they looked, well, so fierce."

Helen saw Mrs. Donaldson's children sneer at the ridge of tummy poking over their mother's pants. That was it. No baby. Ever. She couldn't have stood a child turning on her quite so sharply. Too many betrayals, as constant as tides. Melissa assured Mrs. Donaldson that seals were more nervous around humans than the other way around and went on to describe the elaborate, bloody dance that led to next year's set of pups. Teeth were used to grasp and clinch; wounds that led to serious scars were common; but Melissa made it sound as pragmatic as calculus, something graphed and understood.

Motoring toward the island with Anne and Dr. Marquand, Helen was unsure if she wanted to be back on land. Last night, Dr. Marquand had told them no one really knew why whales sometimes beached themselves. Viruses might destroy their inner compass, but that was just a guess. Helen was thinking she knew what being directionless felt like, when she heard a shrill honking, sounds utterly at odds with Melissa's clipped descriptions and closest to painful attempts to clear blocked sinuses. The seals.

Helen was ashamed at her pleasure that nature once again proved larger than Melissa's pinched, respectful vocabulary.

Rippling darkness stretched across the beach. Elephant seals of all sizes coated the sand. Males tossed the brown sausage of fat that hung from their noses; females like plump cigars had strewed themselves in messy rows across the beach. But their hind flippers were delicate, spread as slack and graceful as black petals.

In spite of herself, Helen remembered what Melissa told them about the animals: that they did nothing but eat for months on end, then lolled on the beach to tend the pups and recover from the exhausting swim from Alaska. The same route the grays took. All these vast migrations, all these mammals braving the ocean thanks to some old instructions inscribed in their cells. Without realizing it, Helen stopped on the path the others had traced. Her head swam, unused to level land, unused to swarming seals, some still with their pups' snub noses attached to the firm bulb of a nipple. The babies didn't let go for a second. Plugged into their mothers, they trained their dark eyes on Helen. Even the mothers stopped their squeals as they watched her try to pick her way quickly through the honking nursery.

As Helen scrambled up the beach, she heard Melissa say, "Cedros has been the home of migrating seals for at least two thousand years." The young woman explained that biologists had used carbon dating on samples of fossilized droppings.

"Imagine coming here and looking for dung as old as Christ," Dr. Marquand mused.

"Do they mate for life?" asked one of the Donaldson children. He cupped a black oval stone.

Dr. Marquand said, "Of course they don't. I have never seen such bedroom eyes. Even the babies have them."

"They remind me of those people on the beach in Cannes," Anne said. "Everyone sort of loose and flabby without a stitch on. Which is sort of awful and kind of great at once."

Dr. Marquand didn't seem as sure about this as Anne, but

Helen glanced back at the seals. For all their flapping, all their fighting, they looked quite at ease. Maybe it was because they didn't have much choice in the matter. Hand on her belly, Helen thought there must be something calm in giving in to your biology.

Dr. Marquand blew his nose loudly in a lawn handkerchief. "It's wrong. It's just wrong. I don't feel right about tramping across breeding grounds."

"They seemed so indifferent, as if they were sorry for us," Helen said.

Tucking in the ends of her kerchief, Anne said, "I felt a little like I'd just walked into someone's house uninvited. Though they were good sports about it."

"That's just it," said Dr. Marquand, "They could give two figs. But they should. Or we should."

Melissa called, "Time for harbor seals, people." She was going to show them a cove where these daintier cousins of elephant seals could sometimes be seen. Helen, Dr. Marquand, and Anne were straggling behind when Anne sniffed the air and said, "Garlic. She didn't say anything about people being here."

"Where's it coming from?" Helen asked and Anne pointed to the top of a dune, where, climbing to the crest, Helen saw a pair of weathered shacks. There was a chicken, its wattle flicking in the wind. Children scampered with a thin dog. When they saw Helen, they froze. Where were their parents? The children broke into motion and dashed inside a shack. The dog yapped once, then trotted off to sit near a pile of tires. Helen noticed diapers on another line. She skidded down the dune to join Anne and Dr. Marquand.

"There are children up there, chickens, a dog," Helen told them. "Diapers on a line."

"People. Not a mention of them," said Dr. Marquand.

"Maybe they poach seal skins and turtle eggs," said Anne.

"Even if they do, don't they deserve a line or two in a brochure?" Helen asked. "A brief mention during pinnaped update?"

"Yes," said Dr. Marquand. "Of course. We'll mention it this evening." He looked tired. They arrived at the cove where harbor seals were supposed to sun themselves, but the day had turned cloudy. The seals had gone.

On the way back to *Atlantis,* Dr. Marquand asked the man piloting their boat if he knew there was a village on Cedros.

"Sure," the man said, "the cook buys lobsters from them." Dr. Marquand glowered. Anne looked drawn as she rubbed her sunglasses clean. Helen's feet were icy and she was relieved that they were heading back to tea and warm bunks.

Then they heard something behind them, shouts from the Donaldsons and Melissa. Mrs. Donaldson was yelling, gripping her tennis hat. Melissa was gesturing for everyone to sit down. For once, Helen thought Melissa was absolutely right. The waves were high.

There were suddenly four whales among them, two cows with calves, circling between the boats. Helen's pilot quieted his engine, maneuvering the craft toward the animals with the precision of a jeweler tipping a stone toward prongs. Helen leaned over the gunwale and saw a huge wavering shadow just below the surface and realized that the forty-foot length was alive, not just shadow, and that it was coming toward her and the boat, which, she was suddenly conscious, was made only of aluminum. It could be crumpled as easily as a can if something deft and sturdy like the fluke of a whale decided to tap it. Then the shadow broke the surface, and the broad nose of a grown whale tipped into the light, and Helen found herself staring into another huge, gray eye that blinked, took her in, and blinked again. With a bubbling sound coming from her blowhole, she went down again and Helen could not bear it.

The motor thrummed, the waves chopped against the side of

the boat. The rubber soles of Dr. Marquand's shoes squeaked against the floor. His breath came hard and fast. Helen heard Melissa try to shout something at them but the wind was blowing too hard. They were on their own here with the whales. The mother surfaced again, now supporting her calf, scratched like her with the same loopy white calligraphy.

Dr. Marquand said, "She's asking us to touch the baby," and they all reached over the edge of the boat and planted their hands on the cool skin. The baby shut his eyes as if to feel their stroking fingers. The skin was so much softer than Helen thought it would be. She could almost dent it, as if it were the flesh of a cactus. And then her fingers felt a layer of something stiff just below the surface, the first sheet of blubber, not flabby but as hard as the tread of a tire. The baby opened his mouth and the shining filaments of his newborn's baleen caught the light. His mother, still submerged, shimmered below. And then they were gone, as abruptly as they'd appeared. Dr. Marquand stretched his hand out to where the animals had been.

Their pilot grinned. The Donaldsons were beaming, too; they also had had a friendly encounter. But Melissa was nervous. This was unexpected. She started waving them back to *Atlantis.*

Then something else went awry. Dr. Marquand turned white. He tilted to starboard and Helen thought wildly for a moment that he was going to take a nap, but he kept falling and tumbled overboard. The boat pitched. Dr. Marquand landed facedown in the water, his legs slightly below the surface. His hat had flown from his head and bobbed on the crest of a wave. Helen launched herself toward him. She had to get to Dr. Marquand before he sank. The boat rocked wildly with the loss of two bodies.

The water sucked at her clothes, made her so heavy she thought she might go under, too. She grabbed him and her fingers brushed against the skin of his neck. His flesh was still warm, although as she tipped his face upward, she knew that wouldn't last for long. Her eyes blurred with salt, then cleared. Anne shouted, her mouth a sad, small *O*. The pilot tried to start the engine, which chugged and died.

Helen and Dr. Marquand floated further from the boat, although she was not concerned with that right now. Her teeth clattered and her arms trembled, but she wanted to smooth his white hair to his forehead before that long-armed man hoisted him up as if he were no more than a net of tuna. She churned her feet as she wove her arms through his. Most of all, she tried to keep his head out of the water. He would have hated to be seen like that.

He weighed so much. She paddled madly. She wasn't, she realized, equipped for long migrations or underwater birth. Helen was barely afloat. But as she cradled him, she felt the ring of her own pulse in her wrist. A plank of wood that could have come from an old pier floated past them. The engine caught. The boat moved toward them. Her lips against the cold shell of his ear, she told him if a baby were there, she would let it stay.

accidentals

ALICE STARTED WORK AT THE WAWA STREET HOME TWO YEARS ago, the same week Conrad—muttering, tattered, and bony—moved there from Met State. Peering at Alice between wide feathers of stogie smoke, he announced he would refer to her only as the "Kennedy lesbian." Alice, neither Kennedy nor lesbian, smiled a plucky smile, waved away the smoke and thought, My God, what am I doing here? But staff members loved it, and the epithet was soon reduced to initials in the patient log, as in "Conrad ran through kitchen, shouting that the K.L. was in hot pursuit." Now, Alice liked the nickname. Conrad's wild, unsolvable strangeness had singled her out from the start.

Tonight, however, Alice wanted to demand something impossible, like a fragment of conversation, which meant it was time to retreat to the office. "Night, Conrad," she said, not even caring if she'd hit the counselor's goal, that elusive neutral tone. In answer, he ground out his fifth cigar of the evening and started to hum.

Once the door was shut, she switched the coffee brewer's setting to "full bodied and dark." A poster illustrating the Heimlich was stuck to a wall, but two of the corners had lost their tape and rolled up to cover crucial information. Alice clutched her throat in the International Choking Gesture and watched her reflection in the window of the office, a cozy spot on the first floor. The Wawa Street Home was a squat Victorian in West Philadelphia with gaps as frank as missing fingers in its gingerbread. Wondering how the Gesture had become International, Alice opened the log, ragged and bulky with years of observation. In spite of all that noticing, no one had ever found a succinct way to describe things as subtle as the flickers of mood that lighted Claude's face when he talked about his ex-wife. Instead, Alice focused on a list of times medications were taken, the pretty names of the drugs sounding like lovers in an Italian opera. Stellazine and Klonopin, the ill-starred pair, Haldol the tyrannical father. Ends of shifts could make Alice feel a little flighty.

Stanislaus swung into the room and suddenly things felt solid again. His fat bunch of keys glittered in the lamplight. He showed Alice a pair of loafers he'd just bought. Nigerian, serene, and cheerful, he held a second fulltime job at Stern's, as the shoe manager. Stanislaus's entries in the log contained more "things just fine" than one would think possible at a residence for chronics. But somehow it seemed plausible that with Stanislaus in charge, things were fine. For a while at least.

"How you doing?" he asked.

"Just fine," Alice said. She pulled on her rain slicker. No one believed her these days. Her father had died eight months ago. She had money now, though no one at Wawa knew how much. Since adolescence, Alice had cultivated a certain edgy jauntiness, incompatible with the idea of inheritance. Especially one large enough to earn an extra degree entitling her to lab coats and clipboards. Enough, even, to buy her own house and keep neighbors a large lawn away and still she was here, watching the loons.

Watching Stanislaus focus on his shift rituals—hanging his jacket, slipping a pen in his shirt pocket—Alice remembered arriving in Philadelphia from D.C. She'd just left her first job after college, as a paralegal for a trio of muted attorneys. Her father had found the position for her, and she'd felt guilty not being able to give a better reason for quitting than that she had terrible nightmares about being locked in the copy room with the partners.

"Where will you go?" he asked, and she blurted, without knowing why, "Philadelphia." She'd always liked the city's long, soft name. It had felt wonderful, that hour and a half on the train going north, free and anxious, moving.

Fortunately, she'd liked the city, its grit and motley sprawl pleasing after the capital's strict geography. Sitting on the rim of a partly tiled fountain in Rittenhouse Square, circling want ads, Alice had let herself imagine working in everything from libraries to pet stores. Then she'd seen the notice for the halfway house. Flexible hours, it said. Supportive environment. The fountain sprinkled the newspaper, blurring the phone number, but after one wrong call, Alice got through to the Wawa. "The what?" her mother said when Alice called California to announce her new job. "Alice, how much money do you need?"

But her father, from his tidy office in New York, had listened to his daughter describe who sat where during group meeting and who could be trusted with matches. Alice's lack of experience worried the director at first, but everyone said she was a natural. "It sounds like you're enjoying yourself," her father said finally.

"Yes," Alice answered, surprised. "I am."

"That's important," he told her. "Don't underestimate pleasure." And while she would never have called her work pleasurable, it was still, even two years later, satisfying. Even so, Alice was not completely clear about why she stayed. It might have had something to do with knowing she'd become able to read the progress of craziness, as if it were a flight pattern, full of wobbly green blips on a screen. It might have been the work's scruffy honesty. It was something she could have talked about with her father, a subject they would have handled delicately, with bemusement.

Stanislaus put his shoes in a cubby and cocked his head, drawing Alice back to the office, the smell of burned coffee. "He's at it again," said Stanislaus. Alice cracked open the door. It was Conrad, chanting: "Lorenz, Pavlov, Conrad Brown, Leakey, and, perhaps, a few hundred others." Two weeks, at the outside. They should start angling for a room at the Institute now; beds were in short supply. "Ten days, four dollars," said Stanislaus. He fished a fedora from the file cabinet. The hat was the Loon Pool, in which everyone but the director participated. Vicky believed that with therapy, patience, and a judicious use of medication, mental illness Could Be Overcome. She was touching, really. Still, they kept the hat in the drawer.

"How can he know all the names of all the Nobel Prize physicists ever and then say he can't tell time?" Alice wondered aloud. Not only that. Conrad noticed the tiniest details—a hem tacked up with safety pins, the changed level of a ketchup bottle—but wrote papers on the fact that China was a hoax.

"That man is crazier than a bug," said Stanislaus, who translated sometimes, Alice suspected, from idioms in his native Ibo, which seemed to have a richer range than English for describing unbalanced states of mind. A breeze that smelled of the Delaware blew through the screen. Her shift well over, Alice found herself about to pour a cup of coffee, when Stanislaus said, "Alice. Go home."

It was still light enough for Alice to walk back across the river. It was Philadelphia's most beautiful spring in years, as green and cool as unripe pears. The train station was newly gilded. The *Inquirer* was printing poems. Falcons, released to control vermin, were thriving: they nested on bridges and, when hungry, swept down to seize the fussy pigeons of Rittenhouse Square. Alice had seen a photo of it. A streak of gray speed that split a cloud of rock doves. It didn't seem fair to set the world's fastest bird against a pigeon. Walking past beds of hosta and stone lions, it was hard to believe that Philadelphia could foster such a predatory wildness.

Alice lived off the square in a brownstone, a home one of its inheritors had carved into ten oddly shaped apartments. Tonight, she lay on her sofa and stroked the patches where the brown velvet had been rubbed bald. It was a castoff of her father's and he had called it, in his dated way, a davenport. He had died of a stroke, falling from the wing chair in his apartment on a tree-lined street in New York. The cleaning woman told Alice he had been reading the *Times.* She'd flushed as she'd said this, and Alice wondered if there'd been something the woman wasn't saying. It was hard to imagine her father in anything less than perfect order. Tie correctly dimpled, socks pulled taut over ankles.

Nothing obvious had changed since he'd died; she'd kept going, a bit numb, but still moving, not exactly well but not destroyed. It was only slightly worse than the year when she was five and her mother had plucked her from New York and moved to California. Neither parent seemed particularly angry or even sad at the event. Everyone remained quite calm and cheerful, as if divorce were nothing more than a freakish storm that had blown them to opposite coasts.

Summers, the wind shifted and Alice found herself on a polite island off the coast of Maine where a fluttering buffer of aunts set itself between her and her father. Now and then the aunts took naps and he would take her sailing. She was always glad when rope creaked in the tackles and wind pummeled the mainsail: it made it hard to talk. On breezeless days, he would ask decorous questions. Was she having a good time? Did she enjoy her cousins? He seemed more like a vague relation from a remote and mannered time than a father. A gentleman who'd survived a terrible war. She had liked him better after thinking that. It meant his silence wasn't awkwardness with her, but a sign of some manly restraint. Even as she grew older and practiced a certain abruptness of style, darting from college to college, city to city, his kind and scrupulous reserve had never wavered.

Alice's floor boards shivered. A couple had just moved in next door. She had seen the new tenants in the hall last night, toting neatly sealed boxes. She was sure they hosted brunches with rounds of French cheese and crisp white wines. Pale and stylish people. Alice turned the TV on to block the pounding of nails on the other side of the wall. "Why do they bother me?" Alice asked herself aloud, the habit leaking over from work. The apartment had stayed empty for months and Alice had grown used to talking at the TV, singing jingles, reminding herself of errands and bills. With two new sets of ears ten inches away, she'd be much more shy. Schiff/Macalester the label on the mailbox said; it was printed in an architect's block letters.

Her father's handwriting had been like that, careful, stylized. Since the memorial service, Alice hadn't been back to the city. The key to the apartment sat in a glass bowl on a table next to the sofa, jumbled among tokens and paper clips. Letters from a New York law firm stood in a stack next to it. Alice's fist came down on the tabletop, and to her surprise, the tremor sent the bowl to the floor, where it broke in a loud, wild spray. There was a pause in the angular bustle through the wall, the gathering of an apprehension, as if everyone were listening for what would happen next.

The only thing that's happening in my life, Alice thought the next morning, is that I am always late to work. She crept in to the staff meeting just in time to hear Vicky describe something she was calling a New Tradition: birthday parties for the residents. Conrad was turning forty-five this week, though thanks to the rough chemistry of nicotine and psychotropic drugs he passed easily for seventy. Alice would have liked to say that New Tradition sounded more like a panty liner than a fête, but her lateness would have leant the remark a sour edge.

Vicky gave Marissa credit for the idea. Marissa's pet topic, so far mercifully ignored, was a cleaning calendar. She thought it inappropriate when Alice played Crazy Eights with Claude and Eddie. Stanislaus called Marissa "The Broom."

Alice opened the second drawer of the file cabinet, the home of Conrad's folder, as awkward and battered as Wawa's copy of the yellow pages. "Conrad thinks he's immortal, it says here about a thousand times. Birthdays don't mean anything to him," she said.

Clinical reasons aside, Alice found Conrad's obvious distance from the festive tone of birthdays depressing. Aloud, she added he seemed to be gearing up for an episode.

"Was he quiet last night, Stanislaus?" Vicky asked.

Apparently, he'd been fine, though he'd set off a smoke alarm while lighting a cigar beneath it. But he did say he was sorry, Stanislaus noted. Alice could picture the gangly, satiric bow. "Apologies, m'lord," Conrad would mumble.

"People, perhaps we should give it a go," Vicky said. It was a chance, she continued, to build community, which was a bit much even for Vicky, but it made Alice feel chastened and surly, as intended.

With the zeal of the privileged and guilty, Marissa went ahead and baked a cake. Conrad didn't show up, nesting, Alice suspected, next to a wall of Hegel at the public library. Marissa had strung a few strips of crepe paper around the common room, which looked to Alice more like blue arrows pointing at mistakes in the ceiling's paint job. Claude batted a green balloon between his hands. Alan, who got antsy around anything that could pop, slunk to a corner. Everyone lit up. They all smoked generics, except Eddie, who had a job as a bagger at the Great Scot and earned enough for Salems. Marissa guarded her cake, a magnificent castle of chocolate.

Stanislaus came in and gave Claude a high five. "Where's that crazy man?" Claude said loudly, "I want that cake." Conrad was very late. Coffee blotched Marissa's card.

Alice said, "Maybe he'll show up later. Why don't we save him a piece?"

Eddie shouted, "Time to chow!"

Claude turned on the TV and said, "My favorite!" It was a video of men playing guitars perched on their hips more like rifles than instruments. The singer slouched in a field. A knobby Holstein munched grass. Claude began to dance, shimmying around the room, knocking into side tables. "All we need now is pheasant under glass," he yelled as he boogied past.

"Alice, could you tell Claude to stop moving so fast?" Alan asked.

"He's dancing, Alan," she answered. "He's having fun." The cow, still chewing, rose above the field.

"This song reminds me of my mother. She loved this music," he said, looking weepy.

"Your mother liked Def Leppard?" Claude asked.

"Mother, who's talking about my mother?" Eddie shouted, cake on his teeth. He pried two Salems from his pack and shouted they were presents for Conrad and he would chop off the fucking hands of anyone who tried to steal them.

It made Alice happy to think that from the street, there was no reason for anyone to pass this house in the spring twilight and see it as anything but an ordinary house. Anyone could look in from outside and think, things are going well in that house. Besides, they were. People had taken off their coats.

Several balloons sank in a weary flock to the rug. Alice was bending to pick them up when Eddie yelled, "Stomp!" The skins of the balloons squeaked on his sneakers then burst in fast, bright explosions. Stanislaus was there in a moment, pinning Eddie's arms and murmuring "Calm down, Eddie," but Alan was already shrieking, high and helpless, gone.

Alice closed the door and walked toward the Wawa Street bus stop. Wawa. It was supposed to be an Indian word for the Delaware that meant "rushing, rushing." It had always seemed more like the call of a lost Canada goose to Alice. "Wawa," she said, and it sounded forlorn in the warm air. The smell of asphalt and cigarettes in the bus had the same stink as the psych emergency room, where both Alan and Eddie had spent the evening.

Eddie had been laid off a week ago but was too ashamed to tell anyone. Alan had to be dragged from the bathroom, fogged and sopping thanks to a bout of handwashing. Alice returned from the hospital to give people their evening meds, and a stuporous calm descended on the house. Marissa picked up the ruins of her cake and cried in front of the residents, who stared at her, sleepy and disbelieving. Conrad hadn't come back. But there had been worse nights. At least they hadn't needed to call the police. Alice picked a livid scrap of balloon from the hem of her jeans. It was her stop.

When she slid her key into the lock, she found herself about to enter not her own apartment but Schiff/Macalester's. The man held a book open on his knees. She saw his expression change from surprise to irritation. "I'm sorry," Alice heard herself say, "my father just died." The expression moved back to surprise. Alice shut the door quickly.

She would have to call the super to have her locks changed. Did their key work in her door, too? Why had she mentioned her father? Alice felt her face burn red. Once her father had told her something that had made her blush like this. Then he'd said kindly that the red patches on her cheeks were like the shape of France. Alice heard murmuring through the shared wall. They, too, would call the super, worried for their privacy, their neighbor's state of mind. She straightened the room, nervous they might want to enter where they weren't supposed to, although she realized, as she tugged open a drawer, there was nothing much to hide.

Eddie and Alan returned the next morning and sat in opposite corners of the common room, imitating sculptures with faint life signs thanks to a slight increase in medication. But when Alice spoke to Eddie's caseworker, she said she could find him a job at Super Fresh. No one knew him there. Things would soon be back to baseline, which was not to say normal. A case in point: that afternoon, Alan ate peanut butter and mustard sandwiches for lunch, his favorite meal.

Conrad still wasn't back. Marissa had stuck notes all around the office asking the counselor on duty to check with local shelters and hospitals. She was too new in the work to realize this just happened sometimes. Conrad just took off occasionally. If someone wanted to fly to Aruba, as Claude had once done—though he'd been deported in a matter of hours—it was well within his civil liberties if not his best interests. Alice had always been curious about where Claude had found the money and what sort of travel agent had sold an obviously crazy man a ticket. She scribbled a Post-it for Marissa saying, don't worry—this happens. It was part of the pattern; sometimes, he sailed just past the edge of the screen.

But two days later, he still wasn't back. Alice badgered the sergeant at the precinct into filing a missing-persons report, an unpleasant task. Conrad showed up at the station from time to time screaming, "Kill the *Wehrmacht!*"

Alice told Marissa that Conrad was now officially lost, though it would probably be more fruitful for the staff to pursue their own search. "Nothing looks like it's missing in his room," Marissa admitted.

Alice sat up straight. "You went into his room?" It was one of Wawa's cardinal rules. Residents were allowed to lock their doors. Staff came in by invitation only.

Marissa blinked. "I didn't open anything," she said. "I just thought maybe there'd be a note."

She might have been right, Alice allowed, although it seemed so wrong to march into Conrad's only private place. Certain territories had to be respected. But as she followed Marissa down the hall to Conrad's door, she wondered if this was one of the reasons she kept working here: that niggling curiosity about how other people lived, the wanting to know more than you were supposed to. Maybe she'd snapped at Marissa because she herself had wanted to open those doors, quite badly.

Still, it felt strange crossing the threshold. The room was neat, the bed made with a plaid comforter that was not regulation Wawa issue. Where had he found it? They would never know and there it was: thick and blue and red. "He likes birds," Marissa said and lifted a worn copy of *Peterson's Guide to Eastern Birds* from the desk. Yellow strips of paper poked up from the pages. Alice flipped it open. The strips were concentrated in the Accidentals section, birds that had escaped from zoos or been blown by storms and tricky winds from the other side of the world. Flamingos in Detroit and that sort of thing. "Can I?" Marissa asked, fingering a knob on the bureau.

Alice gave a slow nod. They would be careful, she promised herself. They would leave everything in its place.

Eddie appeared then in the hallway. "You're in Conrad's room," he said. "He's not gonna like that." He wavered there, looking blurry. "Claude said he saw him down at Rittenhouse, scaring the pigeons." Eddie yawned and told Alice that Alan was in the bathroom.

"Marissa," Alice sighed. "Please get Alan out of there. The water bill last month wiped us out." Marissa reluctantly uncurled her finger from the knob.

Alone, Alice stared at the bureau. "I don't want to do it," she said out loud. It didn't mean she was a good person. It was just that she would have hated anyone doing it to her. She had left her apartment spotless, though she'd balanced a bit of paper between the door and the jamb to tell her if Schiff/Macalester had dared to pry. But she'd also forgotten to call the super about changing locks.

She waited for a moment, then leaned over and gently yanked at the bottom drawer. It was full of birdseed that rattled madly as she pulled further. Spherical gold seeds, zebra-striped husks of sunflowers, brown and red specks of grain. She opened the window and looked at the sill, coated with chalky droppings. A dusty twist of a sparrow darted past.

The third drawer, too, was full of seeds. She plunged both hands in and let the kernels shimmer through her fingers. She couldn't bring herself to look at clothes in other drawers. The thought of Conrad's underwear was somehow sad beyond words.

He was on a rant and would come back grimed and blade skinny, quoting Heidegger at the top of his lungs and lighting cigars he didn't finish. The others would retreat to their rooms, as if to wait out a sirocco, while staff would spend three days convincing a shrink that Conrad was indeed a threat to himself and society, and then he'd be inside, doped within minutes, and, when he woke from the drugs, given crayons and paper, unless he told a ward nurse she looked just like Eva Braun.

Alice sank down on the edge of Conrad's bed. Her hand dented his pillow and touching it released some scent of Conrad, the smell of perpetual medication, as distinct as cabbage but different. Sparrow song filtered through the window panes. Had she known, Conrad asked her once, that when you touch the nest of a loon it never returns? Then he'd said, as if the second thought made perfect sense alongside the first, that glass wasn't a true solid. It was nothing more than dense liquid.

Alice called in sick the next morning and barely made the train to New York. Looking out at suburbs, she remembered that she hadn't checked to see if the paper in the door had been disturbed. Nor had she called the super. It came as a relief to realize she had more critical things to think about.

After a bit of jiggling, her father's door opened onto the front hall. First, Alice was conscious only of the sense of dust. Not that anything looked or even smelled fusty. It was just clear that a settling had taken place.

The apartment was handsome, clubby, full of leather sofas. There was a hint of something fastidious, too, in the curtains' elaborate swags and the tiling in the kitchen. Though it was clear a man had lived here, he wasn't a hapless man or one unaware of appearances. It was an apartment whose owner expected to have vases and porcelain examined for signs of wear or grime.

The lawyer referred to the apartment as a problem. He'd counted its liabilities on white fingers—utilities, maintenance, taxes. Quietly nibbling at the inheritance. Capital burning up every day. A decision, he said, had to be reached. He thought Alice cracked. How could anyone be so careless?

Thinking of Wawa, Alice thought the lawyer had a lot to learn about being cracked. Money was all well and good, but Alice would have exchanged toys and trips and dresses for an adult or two who'd let the messier things slip through, even encouraged a breathless, irrational fight now and then. It was the tolerance for chaos that kept her at Wawa more than anything, she thought: there, at least, was room for the inexplicable, the deviant. Her parents had been so tentative on those topics, especially her father. Even the forks here were wrapped in sheaths of felt.

His clothes were also probably still here, just as neatly stowed. In the bedroom, she sat on the bed, but that struck her as a little forward and she moved to the chaise longue. When she'd stayed over, she slept on a sofa in the living room. Her father was so quiet, she'd never even heard running water. She'd never seen him brush his teeth and couldn't now remember their color and shape. In the morning, he'd prepare a tray with toast and juice, then perch on the sofa in his dressing gown to chat with her as she ate. Why couldn't she remember his teeth?

Feeling like she'd unclicked the rope guarding a museum display, Alice edged open a bureau drawer. Bound to sheets of cardboard with a ring of blue paper, the shirts lay there in crisp stacks. Alice picked a yellow one and, sniffing the clean cotton, slipped off the band of paper. She peeled away her sweater and blouse. The fabric almost itched, there was so much starch, but the shirt nearly fit her. Her father had been a small man. She started to cry then and the sound was like a bird's, a bird with something caught in its throat. Alice cried and felt she was looking at herself crying at the same time, which made it impossible to cry deeply.

She stopped, rolled the cuffs, and yanked open another drawer. Suddenly, she began to search, moving through pullovers, handkerchiefs, and balled-up pairs of socks, everything preternaturally neat, as if he had known someone would come snooping, looking to pocket some hidden treasure. To unearth some life whose traces he'd quietly tucked away.

Her head in the closet, her nose full of the smell of his well-buffed shoes, Alice sat down, stunned and heavy with surprise. Fingering the lace of a wing tip, breathing hard, Alice thought how stupid she'd been. In retrospect, it was so obvious. It was the lack of certain things, not their presence. No letters in his papers. No photos of anyone but Alice. But most of all, it had been the deep and quiet gap between them, becoming deeper the older she grew.

Taking off his shirt, she caught a glimpse of herself in the oval of the mirror. She saw the white cups of her bra, the apple-round heft of her breasts. This was probably the only time a woman's breasts had revealed themselves in this room. How strange they should be hers. Alice jerked on her sweater and bundled the yellow shirt in her bag.

Watching New Jersey through scratched glass, Alice wondered if her father had some unacknowledged friend. Had there been a face at the memorial service that looked especially sad? Perhaps there were things he would have liked from the apartment. She remembered then what her father had said just before he mentioned the blush the shape of France. He'd said, with a certain wonder, that he'd never expected her to become a pretty girl. He himself had been such an awkward boy.

Alice sprang from bed before the alarm could blare. On her way out, she bumped into one of the new neighbors at the mailbox, a stiff fan of letters in his hand. As she crossed the street, Alice became aware she wasn't even curious if the man was Schiff or Macalester, kind or suspicious. It didn't matter. There was just so much you could know about most people. Alice walked through the square below a canopy of city birds, watching people cross the park. A breeze ruffled the hair of men marching to jobs entwined with interest rates. A woman led a cascade of dogs on leather leashes.

Then near the fountain, Alice saw Conrad scattering plumes of pigeons as he walked. Everyone gave him plenty of room. He probably smelled fantastically bad. He stopped to talk to particular birds, as if lecturing dim but willing students. Suddenly, from across the square came a long twist of silver ribbon, something lost from a clutch of balloons, kinking its way above the hosta beds. Conrad scowled at it as a crown of pigeons flapped around his head. Through the nervous iridescence of the birds, he shouted: "Falcon! Raptor! Accidental!"

Alice walked toward him. He did stink, reason enough to avoid him, it was true. But it wasn't only that which made people circle away. Conrad was one of the few who grasped that the sky could open and down swoop the fastest creature on earth, even if it looked, at first glance, like ribbon for an invisible gift.

She moved a bit to the side to continue watching him. It would have been simple, even on the brink of enjoyable, to call, "Conrad, it's me, Alice! The Kennedy lesbian!" People, if they'd heard, would have darted even farther out of range. He might have stared right at her and not been able to tell if she were Byron, Lévi-Strauss, or Nixon. But he also might have chosen to know her. She imagined his fierce glare, the grunt, the pointing finger and all that those gestures entailed: a drawing between them of some wavering line of connection.

She realized then, as the spring breeze gathered strength, tossing her hair and flustering the red tulips, that the connection had nothing to do with Wawa. Conrad had spotted her from the start as another accidental. Someone, like her father, who'd gotten blown to a climate that somehow wasn't right. A bird thumped down to seize a crumb at Conrad's feet. Alice glanced at her watch to see how late she was going to be for work, and when she looked back, he was gone. Her legs tensed, ready to bolt after him, until the idea arrived that Conrad wasn't her worry anymore. Alice watched pigeons settle back to their strutting anxiety at the base of the fountain, which the wind, quite powerful now, had curved into another shape entirely. Then she walked into the wind herself, arms spread wide and gathering speed until it seemed she was flying past the trees and statues, caught somewhere between panic and joy, nearly as free as the other birds of Philadelphia.

mercury

THAT GLOW, GRACE THOUGHT FROM HER SEAT ON THE PORCH, that pink and hazy one, had to be Venus. Mercury would be sharp and spiky, not the planet for a hot, still end of summer in the Catskills. Amos, the dog, nudged her sweaty knee. Grace sipped wine she'd poured into a coffee mug, then told Amos that yes, James would be here soon. James, her husband, was driving up from New York and would arrive, as always, on time.

In the field below the house, the llamas, Leon Elwood's latest experiment, began their fussy bleating. Elwood was their nearest neighbor and the man who'd sold them this piece of an Upstate dairy farm. He told Grace the animals' skittish temperaments were signs of intelligence, but Grace thought it was more than that. They resented it a little, this life in a setting so much less dramatic than the Andes.

Next week, James and everyone she knew expected her to return to Manhattan to teach her fourth-grade boys. But this morning, Grace had phoned Mr. Conklin, the head, to say she wasn't coming back. Before he started to bluster, there'd been a spell of shocked silence and Grace thought, "There, you could jump in there and say, actually, I don't mean *this* year." She'd never done anything so hasty in her life. People like her who'd grown up on farms in Illinois were supposed to be patient and strategic, calm through drought and fire. But up here, only the second summer she'd spent in the country since her childhood, she'd become aware that something in her city life had gone dangerously empty. The students weren't the problem. Their purity of focus was admirable: to be as unruly as possible without being sent home by lunch. It was more that her appetite for days with scheduled edges had abruptly died.

It was invigorating, this sudden impulse toward uncertainty, but it was going to be a tricky weekend. Just after Grace spoke to Conklin, James called to say he'd invited the Chiltons. Barney, their black Lab, had just been put to sleep. They needed company. What the hell, Grace had thought. It might be satisfying to fall apart in front of the most zipped-up couple they knew. It was so hot they might not even react when she said, "I am not going back to New York." What she was going to do next and how much it involved James was still unclear. And for someone so pleased about the openness of the future, she'd been thinking a great deal about the past.

Grace felt even less steady when she heard, deep in the valley, the roar of James's Pontiac. Amazingly, city thieves ignored it. James said thieves already drove better cars; they didn't need to break into a wreck. Grace thought James was wrong. Sometimes people just destroyed things. Last year, she killed a lot of bugs for the orderly rows of onions, beets, and squash in her garden. At first, she'd even had murderous plans for the rabbits. This year, however, she let the fencing sag, and they'd eaten everything since peas.

Elwood had an elaborate scheme for their removal he said even vegetarians would approve of, but Grace didn't bother, although his advice was often good. She thought of farmers as people as mute and rawboned as her parents, but Elwood was moody and railed against the weather. Sometimes he wore tie dye, sometimes polo shirts. Unlike James, who always wore oxfords.

Her husband's pale button-down glowed in the dusk, envelopes from banks and brokers clamped under one arm. "Traffic all the way up 17," James said. The son of a judge, he had chosen advertising over politics and had a flair for shampoo slogans. He also read the paper and recycled it. He remembered her mother's birthday. Lucky woman, friends cried.

But this hot and quiet summer, Grace's desire for the unpredictable began to flare. "Let's move to San Francisco," she'd said in July. "Why?" James had asked, "Aren't you happy, Grace?" then looked so sad she couldn't say more. Every time she tried to move toward the subject of possible change, he looked lost. She began to fear that the marriage, like her work, had dried to something rattling and pale.

He came to the porch and kissed her neck. Amos scraped and whined around his legs. Grace sniffed the starch and highway on his shirt, and under that, the subway's staleness. She used to love his scent, but under all the travel could not find it on him now. "You smell like wine," he said. "The Chiltons are a wreck about the dog." James kissed his wife's hair and said, "Not only do you smell like wine, you smell like a field." Grace had lain in the orchard that afternoon, but didn't tell him what it was like listening to a sparrow hector a hawk. She'd tried to translate experiences like that before and he would smile and say, "My farm girl." After James went to get clean, Grace found herself pouring more wine and thinking about the first time they'd seen this land, two years ago, at the end of October.

The ground of the orchard was spongy with fallen fruit. The valley spread itself before them, speckled wedges covered in cows and pine. It was land that had nothing to do with Illinois' brown and sober cultivation, and from the start, Grace liked it. James, too, was fresh with new direction, wanting a place away from shingled houses on Long Island where his parents spent August flushed with gin and sun. Grace watched him on the hillside, already stiff with ownership, a weekend pioneer.

Elwood noticed her look and she glanced away, ashamed to be seen judging. While James walked the boundaries that marked Elwood's land from what could be theirs, he said, "I saw a panther up here, last spring." Grace didn't believe him, but she imagined it anyway: the black cat, the stunted trees in white flower. Elwood came close; he smelled of cow feed. Then he said, "You got something stuck on your front tooth."

James hadn't noticed the cow feed and said vaguely he thought Elwood seemed close to the land. Grace said he had a lot of nerve. Still, they bought fifty acres and a house that needed a gifted carpenter's attention. Then it turned out James had only to touch a tool to have it lose a crucial piece. He also ran back each afternoon to twist the radio's antenna, as if it were a divining rod, to catch the nearest public station. So that was how the pattern started: Grace came up when school let out, James arrived each Friday, this time with the Chiltons on his heels.

Amos pricked his ears and a growl hummed in his throat. Another car was coming through the hollow. James went out to greet the guests. "Welcome," he sang into the purple dark, where doors slammed and paper bags rustled. Grace followed with a flashlight that bobbed a thin beam toward the Chiltons. This was going to be more complicated than she'd realized. Jane stank of cigarettes, Stuart of whisky. In the kitchen, Grace and James lifted eyebrows at one another and immediately steered large goblets of wine toward their guests.

Having made it to the living room, the Chiltons collapsed in chairs on opposite sides of the room. It usually struck Grace that no one would ever know Jane was from Iowa. She had used New York like a giant hanky to wipe herself clean of nasal vowels. Also in advertising, she wore the severe blond bob of a woman with subordinates. To complete the transformation, she'd married Stuart, who had the long jaw of someone who talked often about money. But tonight, Jane had hiccups that she wasn't trying very hard to hide. Even Stuart looked disturbed; his fair hair stood up in an odd curl on one side of his head.

James began with "I'm so sorry about Barney," which Grace thought was kind if silly, opening the opportunity for Jane to sob.

Stuart drank his wine in such large gulps that Grace had to open a fresh bottle almost instantly. While she was at it, she topped up her mug. They sat there in the hot blue evening, following the predictable curve of Jane's grief: she would take a few ragged breaths, sip her drink, say "He was just such a wonderful animal," and start to shake again. She was curled up against James, who patted her shoulder awkwardly. Stuart sank back in his chair and became glumly drunk. Grace put out some cheese and crackers, which no one ate, and eventually, Jane still sniffing, they agreed they ought to get some sleep.

Grace brought the cheese tray with her to the bedroom. The cheddar had nearly melted onto the crackers and she sat on the bed eating and wondering when she was going to tell James about leaving her job. "You're getting crumbs everywhere," he said, taking off his shirt.

"Umm," said Grace, her mouth full. "I'm hungry."

He sank down next to her and picked up a Triscuit. "This is going to be awful. So much for the weekend. I didn't think it was going to be this bad."

Swallowing, Grace said, "James, are they happy? I mean, do you think they have a good marriage?"

"Of course they're happy," he said, slightly wounded. They were his friends; of course they were happy. "You've got a crumb on your lip. They're just sad about the poor dog."

Grace didn't think so. Something else was going on. Out of alignment herself, she was sensitive to disturbances of balance in other people's lives. James was too tired to keep talking, much less be told about Grace's leaving her job, so they turned out the light. Despite the heat, he tried to curl around her. Once he had her mapped out, he fell asleep, but Grace stayed awake. The planet had set. Elwood's light glowed at the bottom of the valley. She unwound James's arms and arranged herself the way she did when he wasn't there, coiled on her side, pillow flung to the floor.

Then from downstairs, she smelled something that prodded her awake again. Someone was smoking, maybe even in bed. That was certainly more than grief over a dog, no matter how beloved.

Grace turned on her back and wondered who'd introduced Jane and Stuart and how their courtship had proceeded. Was it hasty? Passionate? Or was there something deliberate in it, because they'd known from the start they were meant to be together? James claimed that within minutes he'd been sure, although Grace had always found that implausible. How could he? She hadn't admitted for months how much she'd liked him. Even more, his certainty had made her feel guilty about her own hesitation. And she was wearing yellow, a color she looked awful in. Still, he always said, "It didn't matter. I just knew."

It was in the wake of a pretty wedding. The bride was a knockout, the groom possessed a pair of fine shoulders, but Grace heard rumors that she was in tears minutes before the service and that he'd leapt a bit too eagerly into bachelor festivities. Grace spotted James laughing with the mink-haired bridesmaids. He looked impossibly well adjusted.

She turned her back on their East Coast ease and drank Diet Coke while waiting for a cab to the station. She would have preferred something stronger to blunt the recent conversation with her date, a roommate of the groom's, but the stark lighting of commuter trains and hard liquor might have undone her. The boyfriend had confided, thanks to a lot of champagne, that he thought marriage tantamount to a prison term. Illinois direct, leery of boys who still drank like that after college, she'd said, "Well, I guess that means there's no point in spending much more time together." To her horror, he'd agreed right there and taken off in his convertible Rabbit.

James caught sight of Grace and pried himself from the bridesmaids. Had he felt sorry for her standing there alone? He seemed kind; that she'd realized from the start. James replenished her Diet Coke and asked if she was enjoying herself. Grace answered that it had been beautiful weather. Then, recalling that she'd just been dumped, she added, "But I would never have a wedding like this. Food this small makes me nervous." In her agitation, she spilled Diet Coke on herself.

James asked what sort of wedding she would have. Dabbing at the stain—he'd found her a cocktail napkin—she described it: a ceremony on the rolling edge of Iowa, her grandparents' place near the Mississippi. A buffet with big plates. A polka band. Then she looked at him more closely and said, "I just realized you're an usher."

"The bride's my cousin," James said. "But that's OK. I agree totally about the food."

"Your cousin?" Grace said. "How could you let her marry him? He's a bad egg."

"How do you know?" James asked, then said, "You're going to have to take that dress to the cleaners."

"I know," said Grace, "and I can tell about the groom because he's too proud of those big shoulders."

"Oh," said James and offered to drive her home.

They had lunch the next day. Ten months later, she was married to a man whose idea of the Midwest was the American terminal at O'Hare. She had never been so happy. The cousin's marriage hadn't lasted a year.

Grace lay there, wondering what had happened to that young woman. She'd moved out to the West Coast and wasn't in close contact with her family. Was she having fun? Was she seeing other men? Amos came into the room. He panted loudly near her face. "Cut that out, dog," she told him, but he couldn't help himself. Elwood's light went out. Amos settled down to sleep. James breathed evenly beside her, while Grace lay on top of the covers and waited for the sun to rise.

Jane's eyes were a little bloodshot at breakfast, but there was no whiff of secret cigarettes. "What a comfy bed that is," she said, and

Grace thought in her Eden there would be no room for the varnished chat of houseguests. This summer more than ever she wished eastern manners were like high plains' weather, forthright and severe.

James, who appeared to be the only one who'd slept well, emerged from the barn with an armful of yellow signs to replace torn posted notices. "Want to come?" he asked the women. Stuart, looking clubbed by his hangover, held the staple gun morosely.

"No," said Grace. "Let's meet up later." Maybe Stuart would tell James what was going on. She hoped he kept an eye on Stuart—it didn't seem like a good idea to let him be handling tools that could lead to punctures. Then again, James was even less reliable with hardware. Grace sighed and took Jane to the deepest pool on the property, thinking maybe it would be cooler down there. A boulder of shale perched above the water and they let their legs dangle over the edge of the rock. Coins of light dropped through the linden trees on the bank and dappled Jane's face. Something stirred on the other side of the stream and they glimpsed the white flash of a deer's tail, the wishbone of the hind legs. "Oh, gorgeous," said Jane, slumping further.

The peppy mood of breakfast had died almost as soon as it had been born. So they sat there in silence and Grace watched as Amos bounded to the edge of the bone-dry field that edged the stream. When he trotted off to track something invisible and compelling at the center of the stalks, Grace asked him softly, "What is it?"

Jane said, "I don't know, Grace. I just don't know." What have I started? thought Grace, then Jane dipped her head and said, "Stuart's having an affair. With the vet."

"Oh, God," said Grace, surprised to hear that word from her mouth, as if God could do something to keep Stuart from straying. Really she was surprised. It was hard to imagine Stuart having the energy or guile required to philander.

"Did you just find out?" Grace asked. James would be horrified. He'd say something like, "I'll have to look at Stuart in a new context," yet they'd probably continue to play tennis.

"How awful, how could he—" Grace stumbled toward consolation. "Jane, why are you here? Why on earth did you come for the weekend?"

"I just found out on the way up. We were talking about Barney. I couldn't face his being sick so Stuart took him to a new vet, and I'd ask, so how is Dr. Schmidt, and Stuart would say, 'Oh fine, seems very competent.'" Jane imitated Stuart's plump, executive voice. "And then yesterday he said, 'Susanna says he felt no pain,' and I said, 'Who's Susanna?' and the whole thing sort of came out."

Jane was not quite crying. With boys past a certain age, it was better to help them not to cry in public, and Grace sensed Jane did not want to fall apart again, that circumstances placed her in this precarious situation but that Grace should help her stay intact. So she said, "Watch out for that hornet." To Grace's amazement, Jane looked up, grabbed the insect, and crushed it in her hand.

"My brothers used to dare me to do that when we were little," Jane said and tried to smile. She rubbed the mashed bug on the boulder.

Amos bounded out then from the field, with Elwood—tall, dark, and in a Sierra Club cap—meandering along behind him. "Hey, Grace," he called, knocking Amos with a tap of his foot, since he knew the dog liked this better than a pat. Amos looked happy and Grace, sniffing suspiciously, could tell he'd rolled himself in something unspeakable.

"You awful dog," Grace said, relieved to see Elwood. "Leon, this is Jane." It was easier to hold yourself together when you had to be polite, though crushing the hornet had restored Jane somewhat. The women scrambled down. Elwood and Jane shook hands and eyed each other. Jane tucked her hair behind her ears.

"Grace, I want to mow the upper meadow so I can start pulling out some more of those rocks," Elwood said. "You mind if I do it this weekend?"

"No, that's fine," Grace answered. Elwood was hauling boulders out all over the place, for no particular reason Grace could see, but it was interesting to watch him do it. It was sweaty work: the tractor strained, chains slipped. More than the effort, though, Grace admired that he'd dare to make such drastic changes in the profile of a field.

Elwood said to Jane, "You live in the city?" as if he'd broached something as personal and touchy as the state of her health.

Jane said, "Not originally. I grew up on a hog farm in Iowa." Grace was floored. A willing affiliation with not just dirt, but the dirt of pigs.

"Just like Grace, a farm girl moved to town. Except your dad doesn't raise hogs. What is it?"

"Corn and cattle and it isn't just my dad," Grace said.

"Want to come look at the barn?" Elwood asked. "I've got three gorgeous Landrace sows."

"Sure," said Jane. "I want to hear about those llamas, too."

The pigs were enormous and unhappy in the heat. With the ball of his thumb, Elwood covered most of the hole at the end of the hose so the water sprayed in an arching fan above the animals. It became a screen for rainbows and Jane passed her arm through bands of indigo and red. The sows batted their lashes and gave delicate squeals. Jane reminisced about cutting umbilical cords from piglets.

Grace thought Jane should try that with a Black Angus and could not believe that even silently she was indulging in agricultural one-upmanship with Jane, of all people. The dog, she realized then, wasn't there and might be molesting Elwood's bantams.

When Grace returned, Jane and Elwood were still trading tales of pigs loved, pigs fattened, pigs slaughtered. Amos started to whine. He'd been nabbed at the door of the coop. His collar bit into Grace's fingers. He smelled like he'd become the something rotten he had rolled in. Grace said, "Elwood, would you mind spraying the dog?"

As she prepared for the evening, Grace asked herself if Elwood really meant to catch her full in the face. It hurt at first, the hard fingers of the water on her skin and then felt wonderful, though she'd shouted in surprise and irritation.

"Sorry, Grace," said Elwood, and Grace wondered if he remembered the time this June when they cut a piece of plywood on his table saw. She held the plane of wood steady as he guided the blade through the plank that was almost pink it was so freshly made. When one piece dropped to the floor on a heap of dust, Grace lifted her arms and felt the saw's vibrations still ringing in her wrists and elbows. She described the sensation to Elwood and he said, "Attraction. That's what attraction feels like." He hadn't looked at her as he said this but she left quickly, not daring to stay in his cool barn on the lightly traveled road.

Grace pulled on a dry and wrinkled pair of pants. She sat on the bed, one shoe on, the other mysteriously gone, when James came in and said, "Grace, we have a problem." So Stuart had told him and Grace tried to guess how caustically Jane was sketched, how rueful Stuart seemed.

"I know," she said, "Jane told me."

"How could he!" James said, his hands in fists. "Poor Jane. First Barney, now Stuart." So they won't play tennis, Grace thought. Sometimes James's sense of moral boundaries was as strict as his sense of property lines. She remembered, for the first time in a long time, how he made her learn her marriage vows months early so they would sound absolutely clear in the church.

"James," she said, "do you remember the wedding? Do you remember how hot it was? How it was just like this?"

"Why are you talking about the wedding, Grace?" James

started banging bureau drawers. "I bumped into Elwood at the Agway and invited him for dinner." He picked out a pair of socks whose dye hadn't held in the farm's hard water.

"Good Lord," said Grace, still sunk in the bed. This was the second time today she'd mentioned divinity, though it was hard to say exactly why. "Have you spent a lot of time with him, James? He's not like some arrowhead that turned up in the garden. He's a strange man."

"I did it before Stuart told me. I thought it would easier tonight with one of the neighbors around."

"Our only neighbor," she said as if to emphasize to her husband, this is the man you leave me with when you're away. This is the agent of trouble to whom I expose myself all summer. She found her shoe in the closet but Amos had gnawed away the strap that held the buckle.

"Our only neighbor, then," he said, adjusting his belt. "I just hope he's nice to Jane. I don't like her any more than you do, but we've got to help her out."

Grace stared at her husband. "Wait a minute. Since when don't you like Jane?"

"She's awful for Stuart," he said. "She makes him live this fancy life when all he wants to do is have kids and a dog. I've never liked her."

Was that what Stuart wanted? She'd had no idea. She continued to look at James. Was that all I wanted? Grace wondered. Had she been waiting all summer for James to surprise her?

"And," he continued, "do you think I haven't noticed you've been up here dreaming of leaving?" James was breathing hard. "Do you think I'm that stupid, Grace?" Shirt buttoned, belt cinched, he had nothing left to tighten. "Do you?"

"No, James," she said. She was slightly dizzy. Showing he had noticed was enough, she realized. "It's all right," she wanted to say. "I don't need to go now." But he was too angry to hear that, which she understood. She would tell him tonight. She would even try to get her job back if that would make things right. It was intricate work, slow as the motion of planets, this letting yourself get changed through marriage. She rose to try to turn his collar down, but he stormed out to start the barbecue. Grace found a safety pin for her sandal and followed.

The fields still shimmered with great, steamy warmth. On the porch, Jane had arranged her legs to catch shadows thrown by the flaming hibachi, whose stack of coals James was making much of. She was wearing heels that were quite high. Heat lightning flared on the west hill. In one of the flashes, Grace saw Elwood walking toward the house. "The girls are settled for the night, so I thought I'd come by," Elwood called up to them.

"The girls?" said Stuart. He looked pink, from sun or shame, Grace couldn't tell. A clear hard wall stood between him and Jane, and Grace imagined the list of dividable items scrolling through their minds. No, only through Jane's. James was right. Stuart didn't look like someone scheming to keep a house. He looked as desperate for truce as a dog, terribly embarrassed.

"The cows and heifers, Stuart," Jane said. "All fed and happy. Hello, Leon." She passed Elwood a tray of crudités.

"Thanks. Pretty shirt," Elwood said and settled himself next to her.

"So," said Stuart, rolling a beer bottle between his palms, "you two have met?"

"I took Jane down to the stream and we bumped into each other there," Grace said and passed the crudités to Stuart. He leaned forward to plunge a carrot stick into the dip, then sat back abruptly as if forgetting, now that the vegetable was coated, what he was supposed to do.

"We sprayed pigs together this afternoon," Jane said, "making sure they stayed cool. You look red, Stuart."

James stuck out his hand like a pitchfork and said to Elwood, "Glad you could make it."

"Hi, James," Elwood said, and absently shook James's hand,

then turned back to the carrots. He stuck the tip of his pinkie in the dip and licked it. Even Jane frowned a little at that.

"What can I get you?" James asked. Elwood requested a big glass of Chardonnay.

"Like some Brie?" Stuart said, leaning forward to look Elwood in the eye.

Elwood popped a slab into his mouth. "So what do you do in the city? Amass a little filthy lucre?" The pyramid of coals in the barbecue crumbled, flamed, sent up a plume of ash. James clattered away with tongs at the grill.

Jane said, "Stuart's with Chemical."

"And Jane writes ads," James said.

Elwood pointed at Jane with a spear of celery and said, "Ads. Any I might know?"

James said, "Did you see the Kleenex spots on TV last winter? Those were Jane's."

"Let it blow, let it blow?" Elwood quoted. "No shit." Jane dipped her head modestly. "One of the worst ever," said Elwood. "But I remember it. Anyone like a cigarette?" and he patted the pocket of his shirt.

"I'll have one," Jane said and let Elwood light it for her. She inhaled shakily.

James said, "I think it's time to put the shish kebobs on. Actually, Grace, I think I need a little lighter fluid." Grace decided now was not the time to tell him it was a bad idea to use lighter fluid on a fire that was already burning and passed James the can. In the orange light that flamed, Grace looked at the faces on the porch, Jane wire-bright with tension, Stuart soggy with remorse. Elwood hummed, tapping his fingers on the rim of his wine glass. He smiled at her. Everyone was sweating.

The evening was spilling like quicksilver from a broken thermometer. There wasn't much you could do when that happened, but Grace realized it was up to her to make sure at least it didn't contaminate more than it had to. James deserved better. "Leon, do you know what planet that is?" asked Grace and pointed at the pink glow low in the sky.

"Mercury, the planet of the trickster God," said Elwood and swallowed the rest of his wine. "God of merchants, travelers, bankers, charlatans of all sorts. The planet of sudden change."

James dropped the platter of meat. Amos scrambled toward the raw chunks. Jane knocked the vegetables into the peonies. "Goddammit, dog, get out of here!" James yelled. He salvaged four skewers, but Amos raced into the garden with the rest.

Elwood said, "Let's get those shish kebobs from Amos, Jane. I'll just bring along another spot of wine." Jane, her cigarette a red stub, rose from the bench.

The bowl had fallen to the cushion of the peonies and sat there in the glossy leaves, unbroken. Grace laid her hand on Stuart's shoulder and was leaning over to retrieve the vegetables when she saw Jane stumble in her heels and the slow and falling arc of her cigarette. Grace tried to shout, but all she could do was watch Elwood's hand as he tried to keep the tiny brand from landing in the creaking hay.

James wheeled around. Together, he and Grace saw the instant column of flame. The butt hadn't gone far, but then it didn't need to. Grace couldn't move, but James was a dark streak of decision. He stretched the hose to the edge of the field and a broad fan of water hit the fire. It was only then, after smelling wet, charred hay, that Grace was able to stir.

Jane stood at the edge of the field, and Grace couldn't tell if her teeth or her bangles were clattering. "I'm cold," she kept saying, wrapping her arms to her body. James must have sprayed her, too. Elwood, swallowed to the waist by steaming grass said "Shit, you dopes are lucky. Goddamn." He stooped to see if the fire was still alive somewhere and they lost sight of him altogether. Amos barked maniacally.

Then Elwood shouted, "Goddamn llamas!" Grace looked down the meadow and saw that the animals, unhinged by shouts and smoke, had gathered energy to leap their wall. Their foreign bleats filled the air. Elwood crashed toward them, stumbling down the hill in the dark. Stuart left the porch, bringing a blanket for Jane, who let him tuck her in the rough wool and lead her back to the house.

James had sprayed himself as thoroughly as he'd sprayed the patch of burning hay and Jane. His shirt stuck to his chest. His hair was sleek against his skull. "Grace?" he asked. She pried his fingers from the hose. They stood quite close, hips nearly touching, thighs brushed by the wet and smoking grass. Tomorrow, she would teach him how to mow the field to stubble, avoiding the boulders as they did. She'd be patient with him, making sure he knew what could burn him on the tractor. She wouldn't scold him when he jammed the gears, as she knew he would. She had plenty of time. Labor Day had just begun.

monsoon

AS ANNA OPENS THE DOOR TO THE CHANGING ROOM, THE CHLO-rine tingles her nose the way sharp mustard does. Locker doors slam with a hollow crash. She remembers dashing in here after seminars, nearly thin enough to fit inside one of these red cabinets. Almost undressed, one sock still dangling from her foot, she looks at her belly and feels ripe and bulky, a honeydew gone huge. Anna's mother instantly lost the thirty pounds she'd gained with each of her two children, snapping back into shape as fast as a rubber band, but that was back when people smoked and metabolisms ran fast. Anna pats her belly to let the baby know she's fine about the melon feeling, she's glad for it. The baby curls. A woman in a flowered suit waves to her and says, "I didn't expect to see *you* here this morning." She has what Anna's mother would call kimono arms, the skin flapping loose around the bone. Anna waves back.

Afternoons, the water froths with undergraduates, professors, and staff, racing back and forth across the pool in efficient loops of crawl and butterfly. But late mornings seem reserved for those with less pressing schedules: older men and women, retired or between errands, and Anna, in the watery, limbo state of writing a dissertation. Anna feels these worlds are sympathetic, parallel, even though she's not old and pleated like the kind, stale ladies of the pool who have touched her belly with hands as speckled as their tortoise-shell glasses. These women have prophesied the baby's sex and provided their choices for names. Jacob for a boy; Rachel for a girl. They are impressed and slightly skeptical that in her ninth month she still swims.

They started talking to her when she began to show in the fifth, gathering around her, one by one. One woman told her, "I drank straight through each time and every son: over six feet."

Another said, "The first time, now that was special. Harry treated me like some kind of glass ball." She pulled off her bathing cap with a snap of rubber against skin. "But by the third, it was 'Ruth, this had better be the boy.' "

Someone else had a daughter born under a register at Filene's during Christmas shopping. They've all talked about the perfection of the hands and feet. Anna imagines her baby's fingers, plump and tiny stars. No one lets on about children lost, unfinished, insufficient.

They are more than kind, these women. They have also all noticed, glancing at her hands and smiling, that there's no ring. No one's said a word.

In the slow lane, Anna watches the webby reflections of the water dance on the vaulted ceiling. The water, warm today, is its usual unnatural blue, and laps softly against the white sides of the pool. Anna backstrokes to and fro inside the echoing rectangle. She shares the lane with a calm and dreamy woman in a red, draped suit. Everything fades in the warm safeness. Anna is stretched just far enough. Her belly's buoyant. It breaks the surface. She can barely feel it. Anna's nearly asleep when the baby breaks the peace, swims off in another direction.

The motion picks up deep in the library's stacks, where the pages of the British ladies' journals let up their musty smell. Anna's working on ten of the documents, written by colonial wives in India at the turn of the nineteenth century. Most of the books are still bound in tattered leather tooled in gold, and Anna's careful not to let her wet hair dot their fragile pages. For several years, she's been trying to extract her dissertation from these stories, stories about women who ran Sunday schools in jungles, nursed wan phalanxes of soldiers, taught Indians just enough English to obey orders and recite the Lord's Prayer.

When people ask Anna what she's writing on, she's got a tag for it, compact as a vitamin: "domestic imperialism," she says and raises an eyebrow, hoping she looks as if that explained everything. But that doesn't come near to describing how it feels to be pulled into an exotic sea of tales that is actually real, a world academia magically makes respectable enough to write about. Even when the weather's gray, Anna blinks when she comes out of the library. It takes her a moment to realize that the trees are oaks, not palms, that the Square is not Calcutta but an American snarl of traffic to her left.

There's another reason she avoids talking about her work. Even after almost two years of writing, she's had trouble finding a thesis to capture these people. Women who could cross the Ganges at full flood, raise five children, revile their servants, condescend to rajahs—Anna can't find one statement to contain them. After she published an article on the women's response to cholera, her adviser, Anju Srinivasan, said, "Lovely tidbits, Anna, but what's the bloody thing about?" Anju wears a tilak, a sari, and has the chicest, shortest hair of anyone Anna knows. Despite the hair, she is known as Indira on the Charles.

Anna remembers sitting in Anju's study a few weeks ago, waiting for approval on the latest chapter. The sun struck Anju's desktop, littered with framed photos of her neatly bearded husband and their three children. They all had peaceful smiles. The pictures were taken during summer, against dense green. Anna envisioned them seated around a table, passing samosas from a silver platter, complaining about the raita. She was imagining her own child, bald and willful, throwing spoons across the kitchen as the computer hummed, when Anju let out a little sigh.

"Well," she said, looking at Anna over half-moon glasses, "Give it one more go before you have to spend all your time bashing around with an infant." Anju paused. "You've become quite the center of attention in the department. They're all intrigued." Anna thought about the professors with their mops of silver hair, whispering, for once, about a student instead of tenure-committee gossip or *Dix-Huit Brumaire.* Anju swept a finger of dust from one of the photographs and said, "Go on now, burrow in."

So Anna is here, trying to get something done that won't make Anju scream, "Throw it in the recycling bin!" The late afternoon sun floods the corridors like steeped tea. One of her ladies hates the heat, writes, "The weather here is so intense that even spelling *HOT* in capital italics cannot convey the discomfort of life on the Deccan Plain before monsoon." It really must have been awful. They rarely complained.

These women could watch mutely as the faces of their five-year-olds faded while the boats taking them to proper English schools moved toward the horizon. One woman wrote, "It is a joy to know that Reginald will flourish in England's healthier climate," with this entry dated a few months later: "Sister wrote to say that Reggie died of pneumonia in March." And that was all. At first Anna wondered how they survived the thought of their children dying, how they or anyone survived that at all. But then her older brother Pea had died, in a ball of metal and fire in the thin atmosphere over Alaska, and she'd begun to understand how these British strangers might have managed. Anna's mother, Lowell, still called Babe at fifty-five, never flinched: the only sign of pressure after Pea's death was a tightness in her jaw that sometimes wavered with a crazy pulse.

Sometimes Anna thinks Babe would have been at home with the stiff-upper-lipness of the Raj, though she would have laughed at the woman who had cobras lured from the grass to be pickled in vats of brine. Anna shuts the journal and opens up a thick-spined atlas. She stares at the triangle of India, divvied into patches of tropical orange and green under which nine hundred million people live. What does she really know about this place, its people? She's spent years mulling, sometimes napping, over Macauley; handling the flaking pages of the journals; taking notes on films narrated by disembodied British voices. But nothing makes sense of the conquerors' shrill and driven attempts to justify their presence on the plains and in the jungles, their impossibly rigid efforts to stay English in the face of the alien.

Anna shifts in her seat. Not ever having ever been to India always makes her uneasy, especially now. After the baby's born, she'll be stateside, as Anju says, a thought that both reassures and distresses her. But why should she go? Their India was different, she couldn't find it if she went. Their houses aren't standing; there are no documents she needs. These long-dead ladies, these imperial ghosts, have put her off with their terse stories of malaria, snakes, fakirs on beds of nails.

"Anna, first of all there's *quinine,*" said Monroe, her best friend and a fellow graduate student in history. "Second, the only place you're going to see a cobra is in some bazaar for tourists. And I think seeing someone on a bed of nails would be pretty interesting. I mean, don't you want to know how someone gets impervious to pain?" But she and Monroe both know she puts off going because being in the present makes Anna more than a little nervous. India's too big, too real; it would swamp the territory she's mapped out for herself and sweep it out to sea.

The tea-brown light fades, goes black. The leaded panes of the windows rattle in a sudden kicking wind. Rain pours down in heavy cords. An image surges in her brain: in rhododendrons tall as trees, monkeys with black faces and white tails chatter in the branches, nibble on ripe buds, and launch stones at each other. She sees a mass of clouds that moves above them through air as dry and hot as brown paper ready to burst into fire. There's a cluster of huts at a distance from the trees. Anna's aware, looking at the deep cracks in the earth, that she's on the edge of the Deccan Plain and the monsoon is about to hit. The temperature jags downward, and as it falls, a huge wind rises. A drop of rain spits to the ground. Then the rain falls faster, thicker, pummels the earth, churns it to mud. In the racing wind, the cloud lets out sheet after sheet of rain. Suddenly she sees women, Indian women, who pour from the huts, their saris, magenta and green threaded with gold, streaming behind. The rain spatters the loose clothes like spots of black dye, then turns them dark and clinging. Anna hears the clink of their gold bangles as they run, the crackle of their voices. Pale brown mud spatters their hems and cocoa-colored ankles. This is what she sees when she imagines monsoon: ecstatic Indian women, whirling in drenched saris, arms alive with bracelets raised to a black sky.

Anna is too embarrassed at dinner to tell Monroe about this fantasy as they sit at her round table under the green-shaded light. It is so wrong to have this romantic vision of a country that's suffered from exploding chemical plants and assassinated leaders. Like the pictures of the baby's hands, however, it won't leave her.

She's glad Monroe is there to help the picture recede by insisting on the day's details. He's telling her about a fresh slight from his adviser, a frequent topic, comfortable as reruns. They are eating a dinner he has made. Since Anna barred him from stenciling another elephant on the nursery's yellow walls, he compensates with armfuls of groceries, slabs of swordfish or pale filets of sole. When he catches Anna slipping money for the food into his backpack—he spends a lot of his stipend on season tickets for the Celtics—he takes it out and says, "Put it in the fund for the future astronaut."

Although he turned white when the serene and vacant teacher at the Lamaze class asked if he were Anna's birthing partner, he takes his role seriously. He sees part of his responsibility as preparing the baby for life as a Celtic fan and sometimes recites stats at Anna's stomach while she reads about weaning. He's writing his dissertation on the development of organized sports in the nineteenth century and knows a lot of trivia about American culture, including phrenology. Last month, he tried to read Anna's stomach to find out if the child would have the temperament for basketball. But Anna stopped him, pushed his hands away a little more abruptly than she meant to. "You're traveling, Coach," she snapped, startled to find herself so upset.

"Excuse me, Empress," said Monroe. That night, around two, he called and said, "You know, Anna, I don't care that even though I helped find you a rent-control apartment in the center of *Cambridge,* I really don't mind you won't tell me who the father is." There was a pause. "I really don't."

Anna imagined him in his kitchen, dirty white where hers was yellow and green, shirt rumpled, brown hair spiking out above his left eyebrow. It is hard on him when couples in Lamaze class ask if this is their first. "I'm sorry Larry's hurt, Monroe." Bird was on the disabled list again.

"He'll make it back, Anna. I just thought I'd let you know. About that other stuff."

Looking at him mash the peas and brown rice together on his plate, Anna tries not to worry about other stuff, though it's close to impossible not to. She can lose nights imagining the baby won't be whole, that some recessive gene will scramble its skeleton. She sees herself drawn and faded, smelling vaguely of sour milk, jouncing the baby's tender body as she negotiates city curbs with a stroller. She catches herself praying her thanks to the grandfather, with the profile that deserved a coin, for the money that will barely make it possible to keep the baby.

Monroe stops talking and looks at her. "I've crossed the indulgence threshold, right? Thesis trauma can only be rehashed twelve times in one evening?"

"No, look, I'm sorry, it's not that," Anna says, cutting a square out of the fish that she proceeds to halve into triangles.

"Is it the fish? The guy said Julia Child bought three pounds this afternoon," he says, bending down to give the filet a critical look. Its edges have curled with the sweet butter of the sauté. "Oh, I get it. The tawdry realm of single motherhood."

"Disposable or cotton?" Anna cries. Several peas go bouncing off her plate, roll under the stove.

"Can I remind you what happened when you told me you were going to have the baby?" Monroe pours himself some water and says, "You said, 'Monroe, I'm going to have a baby and nobody had better talk me out of it.' Then you burst into tears and said your life was over. I made you couscous and bought a quart of milk. Which you drank."

Anna pokes him in the arm and says, "It's time for the game." As they arrange themselves on the sofa, she remembers why she went out with him for that brief time the first year of graduate school. They had decided quite quickly that people who felt as comfortable as they did wouldn't have much luck as lovers. Otherwise, she would never have had the quiet pleasure of listening to the hectic, clownish voices of the broadcasters and keeping an eye on Monroe. She watches, as the Celtics lose to the Knicks, how the TV throws shadows of the dancing players off his glasses, and how he likes to hold a pillow to his stomach when he watches a game.

All night, the baby performs tiny gymnastics, as if it knows its agility is going to be tested the next day. On the way to the obstetrician, Anna tells her stomach, "Cut that out. That's my bladder you're stepping on." The baby just keeps tap dancing in delicate, insistent steps as Anna hauls herself onto the T. The baby has a will of its own and it's not even born. Anna's both proud and a little uneasy. At least Dr. Howland is satisfied.

Anna's doctor is a woman in her forties who raises champion Irish setters. Sometimes Anna feels she'd better give birth to a blue-ribbon baby or Dr. Howland will be mad. Now, two weeks before she is due, Dr. Howland tells her, "You've gained just the right amount; blood pressure good." Anna is bloomingly healthy.

She's eaten so many whole grains she wonders if the baby will come out smelling like bread. And for all the gyrations of her mind, it's clear her body loves its new condition. Not a dot of acne, and breasts that are finally, amazingly significant. Her body's opened itself happily to this soft invasion. Dr. Howland jots fiercely on Anna's chart. "The baby's slipping nicely into place. Should pop right out."

Usually the doctor's total ease with the animal state of pregnancy makes Anna feel firmer, but today she has to hold back tears. She can't believe it's actually going to happen. She yanks on her clothes and rushes out before she shames herself by asking for an extension.

From the T, Anna heads straight to the pool. A little floating will help. At the bottom of the stairs she drops her keys, an event, in late pregnancy, that can take minutes to respond to. She plants her feet and is about to inch herself down when someone else hands them to her.

At first she thinks it's Michael. He's tall and has the same chlorine-stripped hair, dull and bright at the same time. But it's just another man on his way to the pool. She says thanks and stuffs the keys in her bag. The resemblance is close enough to bring Michael back and she feels her stomach's suddenly risen like warm dough.

Even though he's been gone for months, even though he told her he didn't want to know, Anna wonders if she should try to track him down at the tip of Chile where he's watching dying stars through some vast telescope. She has trouble reconciling South America and astrophysics. In her mind, he's sitting in the metallic dome of an observatory, surrounded by technicians speaking Spanish that's liquid but precise, while penguins, wandered in from the Straits of Magellan, mill around the blinking instruments. She wonders if he's lonely. She wonders if he's met some gifted Chilean astronomer and already named a star for her: La Estrella Rosita del Sur.

He couldn't wait to find his own galaxy but he wasn't ready for a baby, he'd been sure about that. They hadn't known each other long. She'd met him at a party the semester Monroe was off snuffling through baseball archives in Cooperstown. Michael had actually been curious about domestic imperialism and told her he liked her name, a palindrome. Always taken with people brave in the face of the foreign, she'd been impressed with his terse account of storms in the Tierra del Fuego.

Still, he was familiar, clean as the boys she'd learned to sail with. He'd told her about a pair of wild-eyed spinster cousins who had yearly visitations from Emily Dickinson. She told him about the clutch of great uncles who looked like wing chairs bumping into each other when they shook hands. She liked that he never pretended science was exact.

Given that, he might have reacted more temperately when the condom tore at an untoward time of month.

Now she feels a powerful kick, wants to grab someone's hand and say, "There! Did you feel it?" with someone who'll let her be proud of this state her body's gotten into, someone who will help her feel hopeful. But that sort of contact was never part of the agreement. It makes her sad it would be so easy to make this gesture with the ladies of the pool, and she doesn't even know their names.

At first Michael was sober, sympathetic. He put his arms around her and said, "There's a good clinic in Brookline." So had this happened before? How could he be so cool and fertile all at once? It was then she unwound his arms and said, "I'm not sure."

He got upset only once, and Anna had liked him so much better like this. His cheeks had flared pink. "Why are you doing this? Why can't you wait for someone who wants to do this with you?" he hissed at her one afternoon on the Esplanade where people on bikes and skates whizzed by.

Later he called and told her she could go ahead and have it but he'd talked to a lawyer and it was clear he had no obligations. She was quiet on the other end. There wasn't much to say after that. "You don't even know if people in my family get Alzheimer's," he blurted, then trailed off, distant, and, Anna thought, more than a little sad. After they'd hung up, she'd sat there on the floor, knees pulled into her chest, staring at the telephone, wishing she were made of the same numb, white plastic.

Now, at the bottom of the stairs, she wishes she could have told him something more concrete, more correct, something other than "I just can't." But she couldn't get near words to get at the weird deep thrill. The sense that her body was a vessel, firm and flexible and ready. But my family! she had shouted to herself. My colleagues! She imagined smirks and stares, a career permanently crippled.

Then there was the test strip. The instructions in the packet read, "If the strip is blue, the results are positive. You can assume you are pregnant." On a warm Sunday morning, her strip was sapphire. And she was instantly aware of her shaking hands, clean light filtering through the gauzy curtains, the creamy tile. Something knotted in her belly, then unwound. And inside her, a buzzing hum, a something live. The instant before panic touched off a fire in her brain, that had been her first reaction: that it was positive.

In the showers, Anna watches the curved back of an old woman breaking the flow of water from the high faucet. Wet beads run along the strap of her cap as she says to her friend, "And now it's macular degeneration of the retina." She points to her eye and the beads start running along her finger. "And does anyone offer to drive me to the specialist?" Her friend, more varicose, already rinsed, just nods.

Anna lets the hot water pound into her back and tries to be courageous. Will her baby do this to her one day? Let her eyesight degenerate and never offer to do the shopping? Everyone who passes contains dark potential. A blond with bruises the shape of quarters on her arms where a boyfriend might have held her too tightly. A girl so thin her skin's blue as skim milk.

Anna shivers in the water, feels the baby stir, and a pang. She wants nothing more than to walk back to her locker, get dressed, go huddle with the familiar, faded ladies of the Raj, and cook dinner with Monroe. The old circle, before the baby stretched the diameter. Before she'd listened to the dumb, pulsing signal of her body and an intuition that this had been the right thing to do. Instead, she pulls herself out to the pool, with her mother's words strangely in her head: "Lean into it." Babe, as brown and sexless as a twig, has always had stamina.

Last week, Babe had made it clear Anna was expected at Thanksgiving dinner on the North Shore. Anna was surprised her parents seemed so intent on having her seen at eight and a half husbandless months in front of the cousins and neighbors. "And bring Monroe," Anna's mother said. Babe loves Monroe and says things like, "So tell me about the Great Midwest," as if he's just come back from Mauritania. Monroe also likes Babe, likes to study Anna's family and make comments about the more inane the New England nickname, the higher the probability that the family has Mayflower blood. The fact that Anna's grandmother was called "Dodo" is a case in point. *That* was social confidence, he said.

But this year he was going back to Lansing and Anna found herself reflexively following the route to her parents' house. She knew what she'd find: a gleaming table strewn with shellacked and bumpy gourds, linen wings of napkins. From guests, Anna anticipated muffled silence and compressed lips. She wore a brown quilted dress that made her feel like the turkey.

Babe presided at the table, spry in her green suit as she passed cut-glass bowls of cranberry jelly. A vigorous fund raiser for pro-choice candidates, she talked politics with a vengeance. They'd not survived the last election but you would have thought they'd won the White House given the voltage of Babe's smile.

At the other end of the Thanksgiving table, Anna's father, Jack, passed the stuffing. "Jack," Anna thought, sounded like a sail in a stiff wind, but despite the snap of his name, he'd always let Babe take the lead, though he unfailingly remembered which wars to talk about with which uncle and cousin and who liked light and dark. He carved as if he were playing violin, with long, graceful sweeps.

Guests asked politely about Anna's health. She might have been convalescing from the flu. Then the conversation slid to this year's sewage bill and the fine job the new minister was doing at Grace Church. After the meal, the relatives gave her a kiss with papery lips and drifted off to their cars. Anna crammed extra yam into plastic bowls. The warm wake of the turkey was heavy in the kitchen. Babe looked out of the window at Jack talking to Max, a young neighbor wistfully spinning a football. Max hadn't been able to convince Jack to play.

Pea would have played with the boy, even though he hated football. But Pea had been dead for years. Pea, short for his middle name, "Peabody, of course," Monroe once said, and Anna couldn't deny it.

"But you know the sound when you're shelling peas, the little ping on the side of the metal bowl? That was Pea," she told him. Part of him at least. Rheumatic fever crimped his height when he was little, and he was wiry, with red hair and a genius for taking things apart. Once he fed blue dye into Babe's sprinklers and Anna remembered the blue jewels of water studding the hosta.

Anna looked at her mother and suspected she was thinking about Pea, too. The gravy boat in Babe's hands was half-polished smooth, half-gleaming with water. All of a sudden, Babe looked shrunken under her apron.

But after Pea died, it was Jack who'd gone awry. He had walked out blank eyed and grinning from his office on State Street about three months after it happened and hadn't been back since. It had stretched him too far, as if his heart were a ligament that lost its elasticity.

Babe planted the garden with Pea's favorites, bachelor buttons and zinnias, though she'd always said zinnias were gaudy. It was an off year for elections, and instead she sent Anna clippings about grief from various living sections. It was the year Anna decided to study history in graduate school. It was the year she started yelling at her mother.

The pulse in Babe's jaw started up as she looked out the window at her husband. Anna wondered what would happen if her mother let go, if she burst like the monsoon in this mannered New England house. It might sweep them all right into the Atlantic, and Anna wasn't sure if she could stand this happening or if it would be wonderful. Then Babe said, "Anna, what are you going to name this child anyway?"

Babe and Anna watched Max cross the lawn to his house. "Names are very important. I'll never forgive my mother for calling me Babe. At least Pea was only Pea at home," Babe said. She finished drying the silver and looked at Anna. "You're taking those vitamins I gave you, aren't you?"

Anna had tried to hug Babe when she said good-bye, but it was awkward with her stomach. On her way back to Boston, she couldn't lose the picture of her parents standing on the front porch, bravely waving her off with the hollow smile of after holidays. A small green flame standing next to a larger gray smudge, her parents.

Their colors, gray and green, are still swaying in front of her when she gets out to the pool, which today looks menacingly blue and cold. The lifeguards seem even blanker than usual in their poolside chairs, leafing through heavy textbooks on their knees. Tinny music streams from their radio, pings off the cool, white ceiling.

There's a new sign hung on the far wall: it says "No Horseplay" in high white letters on a red field. Anna starts to smile when she sees it, feels something inside uncurl. It would be something to see horseplay froth up the water in this tranquil, sterile place. She wonders how low the play threshold is. Pea would have savored this, would have pressed the passive lifeguards for an exact definition. Once when the family was on vacation in the West Indies, he had bribed the old man tending the stables to give up two of the horses for an afternoon. She was eleven, he was seventeen. Even then she was taller, but she followed him everywhere. So it hadn't seemed strange when he took off the saddles and said they'd be riding bareback. But then he flicked his reins on his horse's neck and steered it to the edge of the ocean.

"Pea, can we do this? Are you sure?" Anna's horse sensed her nervousness, pawed once, twice, at the soft foam.

"Anna, get over it." He'd turned around and smiled, then nudged his brown horse further into the water. She saw the muscles of its hind legs tighten and release as it stepped into the slowly rolling surf. Anna's followed and she lay close on the warm neck, holding the reins in tight.

Through the water, she could see the dark spokes of the legs searching for purchase on the sand. The horses' ears were pricked high. They snuffled in the salt air.

"Pea, I want to go back." She felt her stomach surge, a tingling crescent of fear around her neck. The horse was breathing hard, the slippery muscles under her legs smooth and pulsing, carrying her out toward the navy line of the horizon.

"No going back, Anna," he said to her, quite close, quite soft. Then his horse surged ahead and Anna looked down and saw the legs were leaving the fine sand, and they were swimming, surging through the water on the shining backs of the horses. The water crested over the reins and she was flooded with something sharp and clean. The sun was impossibly bright.

It hadn't ended well. The woman who ran the resort came back early, saw her horses and guests in the ocean and turned brick red, "looking like she was on the brink of some terrorist act," Babe said later. Pea had been shamed by a long public shout while his embarrassed parents stood by on the brown-sugar sand. Anna, just an accomplice, had only been sent to bed early.

Anna looks at the sign again and gets ready to lower herself into the pool. She takes the ladder these days, like the old ladies, lowering herself gently into the water, feeling the chill tingle up her shins. As she starts her scissored backstroke, she thinks Pea had always lived this way, with something live inside him that let him break directly into things. Anna remembers him shouting from the roof of their house that there were four swallows' nests in the chimney. Then a tile skidded and he spent a month in traction, where he learned Morse code to trade dirty jokes with the veteran sharing his room. "Oh, for God's sake, Pea!" Babe would say, half-exasperated, half-pleased. He batted back and forth across the country, working odd jobs until he discovered flying. He just passed the height requirement for the Air Force and two years later died in a puff of flame a mile above the tundra. He would have loved this baby. He would have been so proud of her. With a start, she realizes she might never have kept the baby if he were still alive.

In the changing room, she is thinking about this, the baby as a signal to her brother, to his liveliness, when she feels something odd. She looks down and finds her feet are sparkling with green sequins sticking as fast as barnacles. She waves her feet and the casual jewels catch the light and glimmer. Scattered on the concrete floor, there are hundreds of the tiny things. They must have sprung loose from the costumes of the synchronized swimmers who probably just finished a meet. Anna wiggles her feet again. She's always liked the swimmers' vivid outfits, as scaled and bright as trout. She likes, too, their serious way of talking about routines with mouths full of hairpins and that they're always slightly out of time to the music. Thanks to them, everyone who walks through the changing room today will go home with emerald-studded feet.

Anna doesn't mind the draft. She feels the terry of the towel on her shoulders and keeps looking at her shining feet. She decides not to go to the library this afternoon; she'll let the journals rest in her carrel. Maybe she'll see Anju and ask her what the start of monsoon is like. She is sure Anju will give her sari a fierce tuck and say, "God, girl, go find out for yourself." As she walks outside into the cold air and feels the baby do its floating acrobatics, Anna thinks maybe she will. It is then her water breaks.

open season

MY FATHER HAD THREE MOODS: WARM, BAKE, AND BROIL, LIKE the dial on a stove. Because we were in honking traffic on the Jersey Turnpike heading from New York to Maryland, it was broil. He hissed, "Watch it, Mac!" at drivers he thought crowded his lane. He jerked his legs and swore when the cat dug its claws into his trousers. He shouted at my sister and me, "Cut that out, house apes," if we shrieked as we pinched each other where it hurt most, on the flap of skin near the armpit. We rolled up our sleeves to see the marks, which were the bluish gray of fresh bruises. Our Thanksgiving blouses would hide them fine. I was ten, my sister nine; too old, my mother said, to be so nasty. New shirts, bruises that didn't show, bagpipes, these things were important to my grandparents, who lived on a high bank, what people on the Eastern Shore called a hill. From the house, you could see the river and fields of soybeans and corn, creaky and dark with geese that the men in the family would spend the weekend trying to shoot.

My father said, not to anyone really, "I *told* Wharton we should have leapt on that deal in Chicago. I must have told him twenty times." We'd heard these things about Wharton a lot lately. My mother kept knitting. From the back seat of the station wagon, I listened to the click of the needles. She could knit through anything—car rides, blackouts, elevators frozen between floors.

"I told that sonofabitch, 'Wharton, that's a sweet set-up. That's instant profit.' "

"Language, Tom," my mother said, and checked to see if she was on a knit or a purl.

"You're not listening," he said to her. "You didn't hear a word I just said." This part was louder.

"I heard perfectly," she said. "Don't raise your voice to me," in the same way she told us not to raise our voices.

My father spoke a lot about the office these days, more than he had when he'd gone there every day. Now, his hair poked up in short brown tufts. Mornings when he'd gone to work, it had been black and slicked down on his neck, as smooth as a wet wing.

As soon as we left the turnpike and started driving on the thinner, more dangerous roads of Delaware, I curled my hands in my lap, away from my sister's skin. It usually happened here. My father's face split with a yawn that stretched his jaw taut. I could see the wedge of his mouth, the wink of a filling in the rear-view mirror. My mother noticed it casually, the way you'd notice the tenth dead raccoon on the side of the road. Her hands kept spiraling the blue wool of some piece of clothing whose use was not yet clear. The pink dome of my father's head sank below the headrest.

We passed a sign that said "Welcome to Maryland" in script as curly as vines. My father snapped on the radio. He slapped his own face. My mother cast off. Deep in the fields, yellow squares of light shone from houses I knew were full of parents who shared the driving and bred friendly dogs.

There were no friendly dogs at my grandparents'. Instead, there was a pair of Chesapeake Bay retrievers, who had gold eyes and wavy fur that left a thin coat of oil on your hands if you touched them. They smelled like swamp. They were called Hector and Ajax.

The car swerved, as if it also felt sleepy and wanted to crawl to the shoulder. My mother said to no one in particular, "The last leg," and bent down, restrained a little by the seatbelt, to put her knitting in a plastic bag. The bag crackled and the cat meowed. "Almost there, pussycat," she said and patted his head hard, so that his neck bobbed up and down. My body swayed against my sister's, and hers against mine. Something fell in the back. None of us turned to see what it was.

On the radio was a commercial for Bon Ami, a cleanser used by Lola, my grandparents' cook. "Bon-n-n- A-m-e-e: you can trust it to scrub with," a woman sang, "Oh, you can trust it to scrub with." My father and I liked Lola very much. She was black and had forearms dusted gray with talcum powder. "We'll see Lola tomorrow," I said, holding the headrest with both hands.

"Lola," he said. "She's a tough bird." He seemed to wake up a little. "You'd have to be to put up with the Laird." This was what he called my grandfather, a man with a beaky nose and flaps of skin for earlobes that he tugged between lighting cigarettes.

"Enough, Tom," my mother said. The Laird was her father.

The headlights lit up the sign to my grandparents' house: it was white with black capital letters that spelled out Pendragon Farm. We would be safe from here. There was only another minute. I had chewed a hole in the back of my father's headrest. A small triangle of plastic stuck to my lip.

The drive curved through fields. The sky was turning blue-black now and there was no moon, but we could hear the geese. Their voices sounded as if they came from under water. When I pressed my face against the window, I could see their bodies in the fields like huddled lumps. The cat, his nose on the vent, started to cry. "He smells the birds," my mother said. We could all smell the birds.

A streak of brown flashed in front of the car. My father jammed on the brakes. Gravel pinged in a sharp way off the windows. "Goddamn it!" my father shouted. "Those goddamn dogs!" It was Hector and Ajax. They were free all night. They were free all day. They had a separate entrance to the Big House, a plastic flap in the kitchen door. Their paw prints painted the kitchen floor and Lola had to sponge up after them. One of the dogs jumped up on the car window, the short claws scratching the glass.

"Oh, it's Hector," my mother said, holding the cat, who had puffed into an orange ball. I didn't know how my mother told the dogs apart, but she could. Everyone in her family knew which was which. To me, they were just wild and ugly.

My father rolled down the window and swung at Hector, who pawed again at the door. "Goddamn dog, get down!" Hector's breath came out in steam that smelled of meat and cattails. My father hit the dog's head, hard, but Hector barked instead of whining. "Stinking dogs!" he shouted. "I'm going to kill those animals one of these days."

"They're just gun dogs," my mother said, as if it explained how Hector and Ajax behaved. Then Hector dropped from the window, yelped once, and they were gone, snapping twigs as they ran back to the woods.

At the Cottage, the house by the river where we always stayed, my father opened the car door with a big push. He stumped across the yard. The cat dashed across the grass toward the woods, a zigzagging streak of orange in the dark-blue light. Small waves slapped against the river bank. "Everyone take a bag until it's all inside," my mother said but my sister and I sat still, as if it were clear to us that the car was, after all, safer than what came next. My father whistled loudly. The sound of geese was everywhere.

"Something must have happened in Florida," my father said the next morning, his whole head inside the Baltimore *Sun*. "Some pressure system." Overnight the air had turned very warm. I was sweaty in my pajamas. All I could see of my father were his large pink hands on the gray-and-white paper. "Have you spoken to your mother?" he asked Mom. The paper didn't move.

"I'll call at 11 o'clock," my mother said, and sipped her coffee. She always called at 11:00 to see when dinner was, even though it was always at 2:00, with drinks in the library at 1:00. This was just the way it was. Everything planned and regular as a day at school: what you wore, who was liked, who wasn't. We weren't, I knew, but I didn't know whose fault it was, though I suspected in some way that it was mine, for being dark and pink like my father. Or maybe it was that he was angry.

My mother was angry these days, too, though nothing she said gave it away. Her spoon rang sharp against the lip of her coffee cup. Since my father stopped going to the office, she drank it without milk, thick and brown. She'd stopped wearing most of her rings because they slipped from her fingers. She fed me toast, with jam but not a lot of margarine. I was getting padded. So was my father; he'd puffed out since he wasn't working, even though there were no crackers in the cupboards. My mother called the refrigerator the "ice box" and it had an echo. She handed out Life Savers as if they were tiny, colorful bombs.

The pockets of my book bag were bumpy with bags of sourballs. They never melted or got smashed because I ate them too fast for that. But it wasn't sweet things that were changing my shape. I didn't eat enough of them for that to happen. My body was changing everywhere, though we didn't talk about it.

My mother handed me a plate of whole-wheat toast. "Where's your sister?" she asked. My mouth was full and I pointed my finger to the ceiling. Upstairs, snipping toes off her Barbie. The hair was already cropped as close as a dead corn field.

My mother sat across from my father and picked up her knitting. The piece of clothing, whatever it was, had gotten a lot bigger overnight.

Dad was wearing his worst and oldest sweater, one he'd owned before she started knitting. He put the paper down and his eyes were crowded and dark, like a room with no lights but lots of furniture. He was very still as he watched my mother. I waited for him to do something he did every year down here, like pound his chest and say, "Love that rare air!" He didn't like it here. He didn't like the Laird, he didn't like the way we had to dress for the

Big House, he didn't like the hunting. Usually, he talked about all this loudly or took us on a walk to skip flat stones on the river.

There was an echo between my parents, like the one in the empty refrigerator. My mother bent her head; the wool she fed on her needles was wrapped tight around her forefinger, where it bit into her skin.

The blinds were rolled all the way up. The house was smooth with gray light. I took my toast and sat on the window seat to watch the river where the current bent and folded the water into gold-brown curves, which looked warm though it wasn't.

My sister came down and was handed more cold toast. Not even looking at the plate, she asked if we could go swimming. My mother looked up from her pattern and said, "You'll have to skinny dip."

The screen door hit the jamb with a smash and my sister and I were at the edge of the river. There was a smell of burning leaves and fish, not a bad smell of fish, but a just-caught, watery smell of fish. We took our pajamas off. Our skin was so white, we could see the pink and blue stalks of our veins. In the rush to get to the water, I had forgotten the new padding on my body, the curves on my hips and chest, and they made me stare. I had never seen the newness in this bright a light, or noticed how it changed my shadow. I punched my sister in the arm and shouted, "Stop looking!" even though she probably wasn't and ran into the water, splashing up gold and gray, my shadow ripped and scattering on the river.

"Fatso!" she shouted back. I heard her wade into the water behind me. I would grab her legs under water when she got over her head.

The water was past my waist when my sister said, "What's that?" We heard a sound like the geese, but higher and with more notes to it. It was my cousin, George, on his bagpipes. George and his sister Astrid had hair that stayed parted and were good at science so their family stayed in the Big House.

When George played, his whole head turned hard and red as an apple. My grandfather made him perform in the front hall, after drinks and before goose. When George was done and breathing really fast, my grandfather patted him over his ear in a way that looked more like a smack than a pat and said, "Well done, lad."

The water was up to my chest. Then the geese started to cry louder than usual and we couldn't hear the bagpipes. The field near my grandparents' house was dark with the birds, but then they started to fly and it looked like a brown and gray carpet slowly being lifted from the ground. Now the sky instead of the field was dark with geese. I saw two brown streaks coming across the dead corn. They swerved to miss the hunting blind. Hector and Ajax.

My sister and I floated closer to each other. The dogs stopped at the bank, noses high. Then one stepped into the river and started to swim toward us. The other followed. The dogs' heads and the tips of their tails were the only things that poked through the surface, their ears like wide petals floating on the water. We started to swim, fast as we could, away from shore, away from them. We said nothing. We kicked the water to froth.

The river tugged harder on my body. We were near the current. I was almost ready to swirl into it and wash up somewhere downstream, at some other family's Thanksgiving, with mud in my ears and sand in my mouth. Anything would be better than being at that table, with those people and that conversation and all that silverware. I stopped swimming and it was almost like the water was a pair of hands on my legs. It would have been so easy to let the current pull us away. Then the dogs were there.

I could see the tiny wet pebbles of the nearest dog's nose. When he was so close his breath made my face warm, I hit him hard, on the head. "Go away, dog!" I hissed. I sounded like my father. My sister whacked the other one, who blinked and started to paddle back to the bank. She nearly beat him there. But the one near me was looking for something to put his mouth around. "Soft as silk," my grandfather said about the dogs' mouths, which were ridged and steamy and had never seemed soft to me. Then the points of his teeth were in my arm and pulling, and he tried to drag me. I wanted to kill him. It leapt in me, knowing this, the way a fish breaks the water's skin. "Goddamn dog," I shouted and I hit him with my other arm. Water splashed up my nose and I started to cough and swear at the same time. My arm had dents in it, no blood, but white dents. Another bruise. But he had left and I thought it was because I'd sworn at him. I had never said "Goddamn" out loud before. "Goddamn," I said again as I swam toward shore. It tasted odd in my mouth, a little like silver tarnished with egg.

My sister had pulled on her pajamas and they stuck to her in wet patches. "Did he bite?" she said. The dogs planted their front paws in the sand and sent a shiver down their backs. Sprays of water fanned off their fur. They panted loudly as if nothing had happened.

The door slammed and my father stood at the top of the porch stairs. I flopped back in the water, my legs streaming out behind me, my hands to my wrists in mud made sharp with broken oyster shells. "Did the dogs do anything?" he said loudly.

His face was bright with heat. I wondered what he could have done anyway. I wondered if he would have waded into the water and ruined his sweater for good to save us. He looked so tired. Floating there, my fingers squelching mud, I didn't know what he would have done. My arm ached. I wanted to be clean.

"No," I said. It was simpler this way. It was simpler to make sure no river mud stayed below my nails, then go and strap on my kilt.

"Have you seen the cat?" he asked.

I hadn't seen the cat. We wouldn't until just before we left. He disappeared in the woods and would have ear mites and a claw wrenched off when he came back. He always got battered down here. "No," I told him, but he wasn't listening. My sister darted past him.

Inside, my mother was on the phone with Grandma. My father was lying down on the cushions of the window seat. His arm covered his eyes and he looked like he might have been asleep, but he wasn't.

"Why don't you take off your sweater?" I asked, wiping mud on my pajamas.

"In the tub, little girl," he said but didn't move.

My mother cupped her hand over the telephone, her last ring clanking on the black plastic, and shouted, "Time for a bath." She said to my grandmother, "I'll tell Tom to get his gear together." When she hung up, she said, "I told Ma you'd shoot with Pa and Gerard after dinner."

"No, I won't," he said and stood up, a little teetery as if the blood weren't quite in his head.

She started cleaning breakfast plates off the table. "Take that sweater off, it's stifling in here," she said.

"No," he said, and walked out onto the porch and then down the riverbank where he sat down. It seemed to hurt his knees. I wanted to go and sit next to him, but my mother said "Into the tub!" meaning it.

In the bathroom upstairs, there was a dented can of Bon Ami and a bristly cleaning brush in the corner. The water was very soft and hot and smelled as if it were the river heated up. I made my sister climb in the front. I wasn't sure what I didn't want her to see; I just didn't want to be seen. I heard the door slam again, hard. My parents' voices rose from downstairs. I told my sister to spin the spigot so the water spouted out louder.

I was getting fat as a goose. I slipped the bar of soap across my chest where it slid up a bank of skin and then down again. It made me shiver. All I wanted was to find my book bag and the sourballs. I wanted to put them all in my mouth at once and feel the sweet marbles shrink and slide, small and tangy, down my throat, but it was time to get dressed.

This year, my mother had found us matching kilts in what she called the "family tartan," Gunn plaid. I thought for a long time this was spelled "gun plaid," which seemed to make sense of my grandfather and uncle. Then I read the label on the skirt.

"Ready?" my mother called. We clattered down. She was fiddling with a gold earring the shape of a dog's head. "Give me a hand with this," she said and let me anchor the cold piece of metal on her earlobe. I looked into the folds and bends of her ear. It was just the right shape for a secret, but I never told her any.

"Where's Dad?" I asked.

"In the car," she said. My mother wore her double row of pearls. She folded up her knitting and put it on the window seat. It was clear this made her sad. "Fingers?" she said. We showed her our hands, scrubbed red at the tips.

My father, still in his sweater, slumped behind the wheel of the station wagon. Usually, for dinners up there he dressed more carefully than for the office. Today he looked as roughed up as the cat after a bad night. "I'll drive, Tom," my mother said. "You can join us once you've changed."

He said, "I'm driving and I'm going to the house now."

"Get out," she said, much louder. Then he started the car and it jerked forward, fast enough for the tires to spit out sprays of pebbles.

We stood there, watching the car go up the hill, the exhaust curling behind it. "Come on," my mother said, sharp as one of her needles. We started to walk quickly up the driveway, but her heels sank a little in the gravel, made her tilt.

We passed the hunting blind, which sat on low stilts in the middle of the field between my grandparents' and the Cottage. The geese had never figured out they shouldn't fly over the blind. Every year, I would listen to a pop rip open the sky, watch a scarf of smoke float over the blind and then jump a little when a bird thumped down, like a dark, heavy pillow. Sometimes the hunters hit it in the feathers of the chest and the stain would spread like a red starfish.

The station wagon was parked with its nose almost in the privet hedge that guarded the Big House. My mother leaned her shoulder against the heavy door with its knocker the shape of a brass bundle of corn. She didn't even stop to fix our hair.

My father was standing by the cart in the library where drinks were poured. The dogs barked when we came in. My mother shoved them aside, without looking. No one told them hush and they sniffed my sister and me, noses deep in our skirts. "Nina?" my grandmother asked. Grandma wore a pink wool dress, belted at the waist. She looked more like a headmistress than the headmistress at my school.

My mother's hand flew to the earring I'd just screwed on. "Tom, could we talk a moment?" she said.

My father poured a stream of whisky in a glass. "Like a drink, Nina?"

"For Christ's sake," Uncle Gerard muttered in a tough way. "Tom, get that sweater off and sit down."

Aunt Rebecca and my cousin Astrid looked at my father, but they didn't say anything. Astrid played with the buckle on her kilt made from the same plaid as mine. My mother's face was as yellow as the paper in the atlas that lay open on the table by the fireplace.

My grandfather coughed and the sound made a current run through the room. He sat behind the card table and started to shuffle his deck. The cards made slow, fat snaps against each other. He took a cigarette, brown at both ends, and made it glow with a small silver lighter. He stopped to look at his cards, slap red on black, put up an ace. Still looking at the cards, he said, lazy, almost bored, "Such a bad example for the children."

"Example?" my father said, breaking the word into three sharp pieces. His cheeks burned brighter. My mother's face looked like it had been torn in two. Then my grandfather laughed, like a human barking. The pleats on his neck shook, then he pulled on his cigarette and stopped making that sound.

My father picked up his drink, looked at it closely, as if he'd found a bug in the ice, then tossed it. We watched the way you'd watch the fall of a goose, but this was gold and glass and liquid, moving sideways. It smashed above the fireplace and burst into sharp feathers of crystal. My father turned and left the room. I could hear his footsteps, fast and soft and fading.

For a second, even the dogs were still. Then my uncle shouted at the children, "To the playroom!" When the door closed, my sister started crying, loud, like a crow. She stopped almost as soon as she started. Astrid and George grabbed the best chairs in the playroom and sulked. My sister and I went to see Lola.

And though grown-ups never went to see her, my father was there. Anyone Lola called Miss This or Mister That stood where wood turned to tile. Lola called my grandmother Mrs. MacFarlane, so as far as I knew, she had never seen her own kitchen.

But Lola pretended it was normal to have my father here. She'd made room for him at the table, even though he was red and breathing hard. "Sit down, chickens," she told us. "Have a cookie." There were lacy oatmeal ones and yellow ones with the single dark eye of a raisin. We stared at our father.

"Hi, girls," he said. We stood near Lola. He had driven off without us. He had thrown a glass. Lola's big stove warmed my back. Lola looked at us and said "Well, now." Later she would turn us slowly around, one hand on our waists, to see how we had changed since we had last seen her. She didn't care what the changes were, she just wanted to make sure she'd seen them.

"Smells good," my father said. The kitchen was full of the dark smell of goose. We never ate turkey at Thanksgiving like everyone else. Instead, we sat down to goose, a bird that my grandfather had shot and the dogs retrieved. Last year, my father broke a tooth on a lead pellet in the meat. My grandmother blamed Lola, but my grandfather was the one to clean the bird.

"I hate goose," I said loudly.

"They'll be missing you, Mr. Tom," Lola said, jerking her head toward the dining room, the library, my grandfather.

"I threw a glass in there, Lola," he said and got up from the table.

Lola put her spoon, tan to the middle with gravy, on the countertop. "Are you feeling all right, Mr. Tom?"

He paced a little. "If that sonofabitch tells you to pick it up, don't. I will pick it up. I broke it. Do not touch it." He stood there then said, "Come here, birds."

Lola said, "Whatever you want, Mr. Tom," and tucked us closer to her.

But he came nearer. "My girls," he said. "My birds." His hand on top of my head felt like a thick hot plate. I smelled him then, the denseness of him, mixed with something sharp and living from Lola, all wrapped together in goose.

He left the kitchen and before Lola could tell me not to, I followed him. He went to my grandfather's office, where the guns lay black and long in a glass-fronted cabinet. My father stood in front of it and the sheet of glass caught his face and a branch of privet bouncing in the wind outside. He took down a rifle and rocked it lightly in his hands. His eyes and face and the gun were shining.

"It's nearly time for George, Dad," I said.

He looked at me, with that crowded look. "You're almost a big girl." The rifle was quiet in his hands.

"No, I'm not," I shouted. "I'm not," and thought maybe if I shouted it again someone would hear.

He walked out toward the field and even though all I wanted to do was run to Lola, I followed him again. I stood there in the wind which pressed my shirt to my chest and watched him head toward the blind. He moved quickly, the nose of the rifle pointing down. As he came closer, the geese did a scared shuffle, and fluttered to another row in the field. He reached the blind and crawled up the short ladder to the opening in its side. I couldn't see him anymore. The blind had swallowed him. Then I heard the dogs.

My sister said Lola was in the library. The only person I could have told was talking to the grown-ups. He's got a gun in there, I tried to whisper to her. He's got a gun. My voice was caught somewhere behind my tongue.

My sister took the plate of cookies into the playroom. At least I could see the blind from there. Astrid and George were still in the best chairs. "Your father doesn't have a job," Astrid said. She was thirteen and fuller of curves than before. She hadn't once mentioned chemistry this year.

I whispered "Shut up" under my breath. George had raided the pantry for empty ginger-ale bottles and stacked them in a shaky green triangle on the table. My sister sucked her thumb. I sat in the window seat. From the corner of my eye, I saw that Astrid's skirt showed a lot of her thighs. I was sure then that she had menstruated.

I had learned the word this year. I decided then I would not menstruate; from the cool way the teacher talked about it, it seemed that this might be possible. But then I wasn't sure if I could do anything about it. I didn't think you could turn it back by swearing or hitting. I tried to imagine my mother having it but all I saw was a starfish stain on her chest, like the geese after they'd been shot. Then I heard it. A boom that if you didn't know better, you would think was thunder.

George's bottles crashed and rolled off the table. I ran out the playroom door to the edge of the field. My mother and uncle were running toward the blind. My grandparents and aunt stopped just where lawn gave way to corn. Lola stood just behind them. The geese had flown up in their great dark sheet again. The noise was everywhere. Then I heard another sound. It was the yelping of a dog.

My father stood by the ladder. He was staring at the dog, lying on its side. It flapped its tail slowly, a large blackish stain on its chest. It whined, a rusty sound. When my uncle pulled his hand away, it was wet and red. Lola said to me, metal in her voice, "Honey, back to the house." But there was a terrible mess down there, nothing she could fix. I ran past her.

My mother's lipstick was gone and so was one of her earrings. Hector's tail stopped flapping. I was sure it was Hector. For the first time I was sure.

My uncle took the gun from my father, whose arms looked like all their muscles had dissolved. My father didn't look angry, he didn't look sad. Clouds padded the sky and took the shine from his face. His hand had sat thick and hot on my hair. I didn't think it would have any temperature at all now. All the heat tilted out of him when he aimed the gun at Hector. I stood there and felt light as a corn husk, white and hollow as the wing bone of a goose. All I wanted was to run to my father and grab his hand and lift off from the field, light as feathers, into the sky.

"Why?" my mother cried, coming alive. She looked ready to grab the gun from my uncle and use it on my father. "Why?" she cried again. The geese were honking but they started to sink toward the field again, not scared enough to stop eating. I started to run, shouting as loud as I could, telling them not to land, to keep the sky dark with their wings, even though I knew that when I stopped yelling, they would wheel right back down to the ground, wings banking against the wind, as if nothing had changed.

mrs. pritchard and mr. watson

THE SUN IN JAMAICA THROWS EVERYTHING INTO RELIEF, WITH a light that seems as tangible as gold or sand. Mrs. Pritchard has never seen her body quite so starkly lit. The freckles on her chest, comets of broken capillaries spiraling across her calves. The scar on her ankle, earned as a girl while tearing round a corner. She'd raced down a corridor in a cotton shift, the cool of a summer night tickling her skin through the cloth. She remembers the spill of blood, black in the half-light, that poured from the cut. It spouted with a kind of generosity, as if her body knew it could tap more. She twitches the pleat of her bathing suit to flick away a trickle of sand that's collected in the fold of the green skirt.

Calypso music bounces down to her from the snack bar. She smells something burning, something with a crisp, almost acid edge, maybe old thatch from one of the bungalows. These are the two signs the day is underway at the Black Moon Inn. The music and the smoke. She stares at the veins of her feet, which remind her of the raised and tangled roots of mangroves.

Except mangroves can expect to live a hundred and fifty years, and in all likelihood, I won't see sixty, she thinks. An illness is staking out her blood. Its name is long and sterile. When she repeats it to herself, she can't believe that something that odd and complicated has shown up in her broad-shouldered, fifty-eight-year-old body. When her doctor, a young man named Kaplan, first told her that the pinch in her neck meant far more than arthritis, she had thought Really, no thank you, I'd rather die of something plain. She will regret her thick hair; the most drastic of the therapies start on her return.

She's supposed to be resting down here, but her sleep is brittle. Everything seems terribly pointed, not calm at all. The creak of a beach chair splinters in her ear. She watches as the first of the leathery women with hair the same startling gold as her sandals constructs her palace on the beach: straw bag, amber bottles of oil, a paperback with a cover embossed in florid, metallic letters. Ravishing in their way, these women, but the conversation that floats across to Mrs. Pritchard is invariably flimsy. All their attention funneled into the preservation of their bodies, a chemist's acumen applied to diet. From her chair, in her tired, unsatisfactory body, Mrs. Pritchard wishes them a harrowing menopause; husbands and children and friends gone wrong.

Will bitterness speed the souring of her blood? The books she and Charles have read all hint at some vague fault on the patient's part. There is always the suggestion that anger, unacknowledged, calcified, malignant, is the problem involved. But Mrs. Pritchard can't remember the last time she turned down a chance to get mad: she's a woman who writes letters to congressmen. A woman who picks up trash on the street and puts it in bins, a woman who looks best while taking control of some philanthropic kind, plump and neat as a chickadee in her two-toned pumps and suit of bouclé knit.

According to the books, the environment of wellness is pastel. There are regimens of meditation, complemented with three making-of-amends a week. "Charles," she'd asked, "what the hell is wheat-grass juice?" But all Mrs. Pritchard had been able to do at first was wail. How odd it had been to hear those terrible sounds coming from her in her clean home, with its gold-framed paintings, its handsome carpets.

Then had come the edgy optimism, the visits to soft-palmed

homeopaths who talked about contaminants lodged deep in her liver and spine. Iyengar yoga. Artful arrangements on windowsills of quartz and malachite, healing stones. A vast and sympathetic empire of those who sold snake oil. She returned then to pink and somber Dr. Kaplan and his difficult news—lots of chemo, syringes the length of kitchen knives—which had launched her on this next stage, this hollow watching. I have turned into an old, sick hawk, she thinks, knowing that close up, hawks are not golden or iconic but scruffy, feathers bent through failed attempts to snag their prey.

She closes her eyes. She listens to her pulse. She wants to leap up on the beach and hurl her book, a hefty biography of Augustine, at those sleek women. Then she wants to dump them from their chairs, see them blinking and tousled, the sand stuck in pale patches to their oiled hides.

But she's too tired. That, her neck, and a blurriness of vision are the twinges that remind her that her body's ill. Her mind has room for little else. Although no one would guess, she thinks, just looking at me, that I am anything more than a normally fading piece of middle-aged goods. She's aware, however, that most women her age don't find themselves staring at the broken-bubble texture of an English muffin, or measuring the pronged shadows cast by forks on tablecloths. Is this sudden attention what it's all about? The skin of her wrist flickers under the skating feet of a sand flea. It started at home in New York. Everything in the house—the nodding roses, Charles's socks—seemed to glow in a spare, Dutch wash of light. Emmy, why is your handwriting legible, Charles asked abruptly, as if it were another symptom.

She's relieved that business has delayed Charles in the city. The extra time gives her a chance to think about why the stained, even teeth of the Korean greengrocer on 78th Street so intrigue her. Then there is that girl she sees on the subway, the one who clutches her black umbrella to her chest as if it were a cat, as if she wished it were a cat. And then there is the inn to absorb, much less the cloudy interior of the island. She is exhausted at the end of every day, although all she has done so far is perch herself on the edge of the ocean, drink fruit juice, and pretend to read—her bookmark has moved a fingernail's width forward.

Down here, Mrs. Pritchard has jolted awake each night around twelve. She dreams of hospitals where Charles wanders down a green corridor. He drags the shiny, awkward apparatus of an IV behind him. Its needle is plunged into his wrist. "What's wrong?" she asks him, but he doesn't answer. The plastic sack is empty and has sucked his voice from him. When this happens, she lies very still in the sheets and listens to the scuffle of lizards in the rafters. This is also the time of night she hears the rumbling laughter of the staff: sober, handsome Jamaicans who nod and say "Good morning, ma'am" as they tug the bedclothes straight and align the knives at place settings. Late in the evening, they gather in the kitchen after the hotel's owner, Miss Carrothers, and her snappish tribe of dogs have gone to bed.

Mrs. Pritchard listens to the laughter, which she is not sure she would have noticed before her illness. It is a complicit sound, full of old jokes and wariness, that comes wafting up to her room. She imagines that the inn's kitchen smells of allspice and bleach. Aprons and jackets would loop on black pegs. The men and women, in regular clothes, lean their elbows on a wooden table, hands curled around squat brown bottles of Jamaican beer. Dominic, Tina, Melita, Joseph. She has no idea of their last names.

Dominic, the head waiter, was the one who fetched her from dinner when Charles called to say his deal was being troublesome. Dominic handed her the phone as if it were a thing of ritual weight. She said "Thank you, Dominic," with equal ceremony. After that, hearing Charles on the other end was a bit of a disappointment. His voice had never been one of his finer qualities. It was low but a little thin, and hearing him apologize, hearing the faint tinge of relief, she wondered why its slightness hadn't irritated her 'til now. Her own voice is her principal beauty. Her impatience with Charles, his fidgety hands, his forgetfulness with the toothpaste cup, all the small and constant irritations of domestic life, why does she feel these only now? Why is this all she notices, not his handsome feet, his tender way with the cat? Being sick has made me pettish, she thinks. An irascible old bird.

Dominic walks across the beach with a pad in his large hand. He has a lovely voice as well. His upright ease is a marvel in the slick, hummocked sand. How is it he does not look ridiculous in a bow tie and white jacket on a beach? His skin is the satiny chestnut of a valued saddle. Mrs. Pritchard loves how he scatters the jeweled blur of hummingbirds that whir above the wedges of the breakfast mangoes.

Now, he makes his morning rounds for the orders of fruit and juice, sweet wet things to keep the guests' skins plump with water. He has stopped to Mrs. Pritchard's right to ask one of the blonds for her choice today. The woman sits up straighter, and arranges her legs so the flesh falls just so. Dominic steps a few feet further off from those who invite potential improprieties. He frowns. He doesn't look at them directly when he says, "Good morning," but stares out over their inconsequential heads. As if his standards of conduct weren't perfectly clear.

It is this clarity that interests Mrs. Pritchard. He is the first person with whom she has felt like talking about her illness, not just its symptoms, but about the knowledge that she has no control over what is happening in her body. She has talked of it so often with doctors and relatives that all the words to describe her condition have turned dry and tasteless. Half the time, she feels like she's describing someone else's problem. She would like to tell Dominic what it's like to know, in your marrow, that dying is invading you and what that does to tastes and sounds, how crowded her head has become with scraps of old events. Why she thinks this particular man can understand this nest in her head she doesn't know.

It is harder to crack the talk open than she imagined. There is such a smoothness to his "Good morning, Mrs. Pritchard. Juice or fruit for you today?" It's the rhythm of a known relationship: waiter to guest, precise as musical notation. His pencil hovers.

"Well, let's see, yes, what shall I have?" Mrs. Pritchard muses, glancing at him. Why does he work for the nasty owner, a woman still proud to call herself Rhodesian? She has stumpy legs and raisin eyes, like those Jack Russells that snarl around her ankles. All those dogs of hers: a pair of setters and an arthritic Doberman, stiff but vicious. Mrs. Pritchard spent an hour last night looking at the creature asleep on the patio, its claws rasping on flagstones.

Mrs. Pritchard & Mr. Watson

"Fruit or juice, Mrs. Pritchard?"

"Actually, I was wondering what your last name was." The words sound plucky, casual, as if she's said simply, "Why, that guava was so delicious yesterday. I'll have some more of that, thanks."

He pauses and frowns, and the same disdainful look he gives the sly, glossy blonds steals over his face. He says, "Watson. My last name is Watson. Would you care for juice?"

"No, thank you, nothing. Thank you." How stupid of her! Why did she intrude like that? He will stare at the sea now instead of looking her in the eye. That is what she has earned by barging in. And he will make her accountable for her mistake, of that she's certain. She roots vaguely in her canvas bag, groping for the protection of dark glasses.

Abruptly she's aware of the sound of feet churning across the beach, impossibly fast. The sound comes from two island boys, black and thin as burned sticks. They run at the lip of the ocean, a streak of fear. The setters tear after them. The dogs are open-mouthed and gaining.

"Good Lord!" cries Mrs. Pritchard, helpless in her beach chair. She shouts, "Dominic, stop them! Stop them!"

"Which ones, Mrs. Pritchard?" he snaps and looks straight at her.

At lunch, Mrs. Pritchard wants to catch a glimpse of Dominic but can't bring herself to remove her sunglasses. She can hear him behind the patio's partition, chiding the other waiters about extra plates for table nine and who ordered the grouper, it's getting cold. Sometimes he raps out orders in patois. That was what he used when he collared the two boys. He held them like a brace of dark birds above the reach of the dogs. Dominic also shouted at the dogs in dialect, and when they wouldn't stop snarling kicked the largest in the chest. It made a padded thud, the heavy shoe meeting bone under dark fur. The animals slunk off and Dominic put the boys down, speaking to them loudly, flatly. They rubbed their toes in the sand, one boy's hand tucked into his armpit, their heads bent. Dominic pointed toward the main building, and, Mrs. Pritchard assumed, the driveway past it, lighted at night by lamps the shape of pineapples.

She wants to turn to one of the other guests and say, "Those dogs were trained!" The animals were ready to rip those little boys to pieces, but they've sniffed and nuzzled Mrs. Pritchard, all tongue and tail.

For a moment, everyone on the beach went completely still. The women let their fat books droop. Teenagers stopped short, surfboards nose up. A man, leaning over to poke seaweed with a branch, watched the whole encounter bent at the waist. It wasn't until Dominic ordered the pair of boys from the beach and strode toward the hotel, kicking sand as he went, that the shouts of the young people rang again in the air. Women smoothed on their creams. The man with the branch flipped a dark, clawed thing up from the beach and started back in surprise.

Mrs. Pritchard's body had frozen, but her skin responded, in its usual, hectic way, flushing the pink of old bricks. She had seen the stain begin on her chest and felt it wash upward to her scalp. Dominic hadn't been able to stay detached either. He had snapped; he'd been fierce. It was not something that happened to him very often, she supposed. Why with her?

Mrs. Pritchard still feels mottled from the morning and accepts more ice water with a tilt of her head, a crescent of a smile. The slim waiter returns it, just as cool. How hateful that things like polite smiles slipped into place when something else entirely was happening inside you. Mrs. Pritchard wraps her cotton sweater more closely to her body.

Carrothers has found Dominic behind the partition. Her dog is limping. What had he done. His voice is taut with patience, strung on the narrow border between the coldly correct and the surly. "Don't use that tone with me, man," the woman shouts. "How dare you abuse my dog!" Mrs. Pritchard cringes. "How dare you?" she cries again. Carrothers couldn't have chosen a better spot in which to humiliate the man. The air on the patio shimmers in silence, just as on the beach. Not a piece of silverware knocks against a plate, not a ring taps a glass. The whole white crowd with its itchy new layer of brown skin pays full, mute attention to Carrothers dressing Dominic down behind the lacy trellis that hides the tubs of dirty china.

When it's over, Mrs. Pritchard retreats to her room. The light that comes through the blinds slices the rug in delicate stripes. Her thoughts feel more ordered here than in the glare of the patio with all its stupid, complicit whites, all its silent, cautious blacks. Invisible, raging Dominic.

To have Dominic snap at me. To have heard that awful woman. Mrs. Pritchard feels lightheaded. To be terminally ill. She says it again to herself: I am terminally ill. It makes her stomach clench as if she were about to get on stage and recite, in a reedy voice: My poem is called "When I Learned I Was Going to Die." She imagines the applause as thin, confused, the lights very bright.

When Mrs. Pritchard wakes up, she feels hollow but solid, like an empty wine bottle. But not as if she's drunk the wine. She feels full of clear, light attention. Her body has granted her the chance to leave the beach. It is time to see some of the island. It strikes her as far-fetched but necessary to find a church. It is Sunday; there may be evening services. She remembers one near the airport: a crumbling foundation, a tin roof that flashed white in the sun. She will take her rental car.

The engine turns over and the tires crackle along the driveway. It's a sound that seems to rattle with possibility. "Ciao," she says to the lot attendant, who looks surprised. She's off to church, for the first time in years.

She must go slowly here; they still drive on the left, an inheritance of British occupation. And while the Jamaicans govern their country, she's read it is the descendants of the old colonials who still own companies here: the Coca Cola plant, the last aluminum refineries. Cars that pass her are sagging American pick-ups, with steering wheels on the left, making right turns something of a production. As she nears Ocho Rios, restaurants familiar from home pop up along the road. But even through the window, she hears the ping of reggae and calypso, sounds that no one has imported. Inside a cloud of dust, children play hopscotch.

She will, she realizes, have to drive back alone in the dark. If she hit someone, it would mean so much more than one casualty. Not only do people crowd the edges of the road, the cars and trucks are stuffed full. There are knots of arms, heads, and elbows popping from the windows. Mrs. Pritchard remembers how she and her sister had crammed red grapes in their mouths, to see who could fit the most. When they exploded with laughter and the grapes burst out, to everyone's disgust, her mother had shrieked, "You frightful pigs!"

"Oh stop," she tells herself. She's leery of memories and of luring an accident by imagining one. I am going to church, I am trying to see something of the island, she says and corrects her steering to avoid an empty gasoline canister in the middle of her lane. She hears a snatch of music from the courtyard of a restaurant. The Blue Parrot. St. Anselm's, the church she remembers, stands directly opposite.

The church has a bell that starts to swing as she crosses the road. It rings a slow five times, a richer sound than Mrs. Pritchard expects. It wavers up and down the road, up the hills and down to the sea. Parishioners politely jostle their way into the church, which, she can see from the yard, has rows of stiff pews painted dark yellow. A wooden sign hangs on the door and announces two Sunday services, one at ten and one at five.

Providence. She got the time right. But as she climbs the stairs, she wants to put her sunglasses on again. She is the only white person, which comes not as a surprise but as a sudden impropriety. She shouldn't be disturbing the things this way. Her skin feels like a disruptive force, the sign of an invasion. She tucks herself in the last pew and makes herself busy with her purse, trying to occupy as little space as she can.

No one else seems to notice her. Nothing ripples outward from the crowd of people come to worship with the Reverend Wilkins. His name, too, was on the sign. As the people ease into their seats and settle their hats—many of the women wear hats with brightly colored veils—Mrs. Pritchard watches the crowd and listens to the pianist, a bony woman in coral, bang out some Bach on the spinet. Women wreathed in fat angle their hips down the aisle. Long young men wear shirts buttoned at the wrist. A troupe of school girls, clutching prayer books stamped with gilt crosses, block the entrance as they look for empty seats. They bend their heads and whisper to one another, the shade of a giggle in their voices. Mrs. Pritchard can't get enough of the girls, the polka-dot handkerchief one of the young men uses to mop his face, the tilted, gauzy row of hats in the front pew.

The pianist has stopped and the Reverend Wilkins steps up to the altar, a heavy wooden table draped in white cloth. Some barely budded gladioli sit in two blue glass vases at either end of the table. The flowers, vivid red, dust the Reverend's white robes with thin, moving shadows. The frames of his glasses wink gold as he lowers his head in silent prayer. A brass cross hangs on the back wall. When he starts to speak, Mrs. Pritchard realizes she can't understand a word. He speaks in English, but the Jamaican lilt is so strong that all the familiar rhythms are disguised. Words like God, sayeth, amen, boom out abruptly from the welter of sound. At least she sits in the back row where no one can see that her lips do not move with the prayers.

If she can't understand the Reverend's words, all she has to do is sit here and watch the light stream through the tall sheets of pale green glass. Church has fallen from her life in bits and pieces, but she discovers as she watches the Anglican service unfold, she has missed it, which makes it even better to be in church and not to understand, to give in to the sweep of ritual. Would she have been a better Hindu or Catholic, with their reservoirs of pageantry? It doesn't matter now; all she is, is Episcopalian, and a lapsed one at that, making the presence of a cool, dim religion in her life even dimmer. Too diluted to earn a service in a church, and she has secretly been planning an opulent memorial buffet, while Gershwin, Porter, and Armstrong play briskly on the stereo.

The pianist has started thumping the spinet again. It is time to sing, but there is no hymnal available. Happily, it is "A Mighty Fortress Is Our God" and by the time she's reached the end of the second phrase, a bulwark never failing, people have turned their heads to see the white woman with the rich dark alto. Oh yes, she can still do it. How nice it feels to let loose a column of sound. The church rings with the hymn. The congregation faces back, their voices swelling toward the altar. The pianist pounds. Reverend Wilkins's white robes stir as if shifted by wind. A spear of gladiolus shivers in its vase.

When the congregation sits again, Mrs. Pritchard strains to hear what is being said. The words still roll past her. She lets herself drift, and an old habit of churchgoing returns to her. She has always had a tendency to remember moments of pure, physical experience in the middle of the most solemn ceremonies. When she and Charles were courting, he dressed her in his roommate's clothes to sneak her into his college library. It was a lark for him and his friends, which they'd found funnier than she had, but she liked the starchy cuffs of the roommate's shirt; she felt almost chic in the fedora.

Once they sneaked past the guard, Charles lost his edgy gaiety and turned reflective. He showed her the carrel where he kept the barricade of information amassed for his thesis on the Crusades. Charles spoke of the books with a reverence she hadn't seen in him before. We are in the Holy Land she felt and was suddenly incredibly interested in being kissed, even ravished in this chilled and scholarly place. It was the first time she had reached to touch him. Weekends when he came to her muddy campus up north, he was the one to take her hand from her glove and massage the blood back into each finger. In the late afternoon light, she took his.

He pulled away. With the jacket slipping over her cuffs, she leaned over to kiss him. It was odd to feel the warmth of his mouth against hers, to smell his wintergreen breath, to have his body so piping, his hands so icy.

It was the act of a brazen woman then, inviting not just a kiss but a man's hands on your body. She would have let him map out the angles of her ribs, the warm hills of her breasts right there under *Life Among the Saracens.* Right there in his sainted library, and it was precisely because it was the sainted library that she wanted this to happen. He pulled away. Someone might see us here, he said. Anyone could come.

Yes, she said, that's right and kissed him again.

He'd said, "Emmy, we should go," and led her back to his room to change. She wondered then if she had lost him, and decided that if he did react badly or didn't think the whole thing sort of funny, he wasn't worth it. But a month later, he proposed, in front of a fire in the library at her parents' house. The red wool of a new sweater itched her collarbone terribly. The memory of the moment so stuns her that when the second hymn starts, "All Spirits That on Earth Do Dwell," she cannot sing.

When the singing is over, Mrs. Pritchard feels rooted to the pew. The service is done. The girls drift out, looking soft in the odd green light. The young men follow them. The slowest are the old women who lift themselves with short, tough sighs. Mrs. Pritchard finally pulls herself away. The Reverend Wilkins is on the steps, greeting parishioners. "Welcome, welcome," he says to Mrs. Pritchard. He grasps her hand as warmly as the others, as casually. His hand, deep chocolate, with skin brushed ashy gray across the knuckles, is warm and dry. His palm is the color of impatiens.

The sky is light pink, with a high skin of pale clouds. More men have gathered at the Blue Parrot, and some women as well. People are talking more raucously. Mrs. Pritchard notices there actually is a parrot, huge and yellow. She thinks its wings must be clipped but then she sees a thong that runs from one of its feet to the table leg. The bird looks dusty, half-asleep. Its beak curves, reminds her of a small thick sickle. Mrs. Pritchard feels the old dread of her illness descend on her shoulders. She wishes Charles were here, to drive, to fold her into bed. She is scratching for her keys in the bottom of her bag when a hand covers hers.

"Mrs. Pritchard." She looks up. It is Dominic. "What were you doing here?" he asks. She feels as if she's trespassed again but then she thinks, I was at church, a perfectly harmless church service. She points to St. Anselm's and says, "There, I was right there."

"I'll take you back to the hotel, if you don't mind," he says. He holds out his hand for her bag, which she hands him reflexively. Dominic fishes out the keys. "Watch your skirt, ma'am," he says as he helps her in. The door slams. She fumbles for the safety belt, and Dominic, in beige pants and a blue shirt, no bow tie in sight, settles himself behind the wheel. The car has one long seat, uninterrupted by a gear box or emergency brake. He has pulled himself completely to the driver's side. Even off duty, especially off duty, he is not open to any irregularities of behavior. He is so clearly in control there is nothing she can do but watch, and there's some relief in this. He's taking her back to where it's safe.

Then as the car gains speed, she starts to wobble with anger. He has pushed her aside and assumed he could get away with it. She gropes for something caustic, something he'll remember, but all that comes is, "How dare you?" Carrothers's words, and now they have also leapt from her mouth.

"How dare you," Dominic says quietly. "How dare you." The car has paused in traffic and they stare at each other. He doesn't move, but Mrs. Pritchard feels the heavy slap of his dislike. They are all the same, she feels him thinking. Every single bloody white bitch. Scratch the surface and it's all the same. She feels her own dislike fly right back. He guns the motor; the car jerks forward. She cannot let him get away with this, with his presumptions. She has tried too hard in her life, but when she says, "You cannot simply force me out of the way!" it sounds like the complaint of a crone. Can he tell I'm sick? she thinks.

"And what are you going to do about it, Mrs. Pritchard? Do you know what 'playing chicken,' down here means? Would you know how to save your hide if some guy came toward you, this time headlights on high, to see who panics first? Would you now, ma'am?"

She is silent, shamed. She has pretended she can wander the island, in charge of an afternoon. But she also wants to yell "Damn it! I'm an old lady! I wanted to get away from hearing that woman tear you apart! From being a guest! Can't you understand it's important to use good hours?" Instead, she says, "Why were you there?"

"It's my half-day off," he says. He drives with vengeful, reckless speed. He skirts potholes and grazes sidewalks. People and poultry flee, unharmed. He drives exceedingly well. At least she won't die in an accident. Once she's sure of this, the anger rises again, even hotter. To be absconded with in this way! To have her car commandeered! It would never have happened if Charles were here. She damns her husband, the porkish men he calls his colleagues, and men in general with their superior, violent ways. She glances at Dominic or should she call him Mr. Watson. His lips are a tight, quivering line. His own anger makes him glow. How much he must hate me, she thinks, suddenly quite calm. How strange it is.

She sees the metal pineapples that announce the entrance to the Black Moon. He slows as if to pull into the driveway. "Are we stopping, Mr. Watson?" she asks. "I have enjoyed the scenery, but I would like to talk about this for a moment." Since her dealings with doctors and lawyers, Mrs. Pritchard has learned a directness of questioning with people who try to steer her from critical details. She rolls down her window and looks at the green hills turning black in the twilight. It is the time of day the French call "between the dog and the wolf." She tells Mr. Watson this, this expression from the middle ages.

"Here the dogs are wolves," he says.

"As we witnessed on the beach today," says Mrs. Pritchard. "Why do you work for a woman like that, Mr. Watson?"

"Do you know what it means to have a job on this island?" His voice rises now and breaks. His supple hands are shaking.

"I don't know a damn thing about this island!" Mrs. Pritchard yells, her voice finally jolting back to its full darkness. "I don't know anything! Show me something! Show me one damn thing!"

"All right," he shouts. For an instant, the car rings with their hot voices. Then the anger dies. Mrs. Pritchard realizes she has not yelled like this since her diagnosis: she has kept herself muted, as if to conserve essential heat. She wonders if he feels this, too. "Do you yell a lot, Mr. Watson? And at white women?"

He turns to her and says dryly, "It doesn't happen often in my line of work." He keeps looking at her. "And you, do you yell at white women?"

"Oh yes," she says, "all the time. Black men aren't exactly in my repertoire, though." How amazing they have dealt with each other like this, at full volume. How strange they bring this out in one another and that they should find each other now.

They drive in silence. Cars, still without headlights even though it's grown dark, lurch past them. Have the other drivers seen that inside this little car there is a sardonic black god and a stumpy white woman heading Lord knows where?

Then it strikes her this is what it means to be alone. To have no one expecting you. It's what Charles will have when she is dead. This kind of separateness is what she will have in the last months, and she guesses that this is what the disease will bring, an occupation of herself, an experience so odd and personal it will not bear translation.

Despite the dark trees and the smell of charring meat, she feels a sort of excitement, something on the line between fear and pleasure. It reminds her of the time she scrambled across an ancient aqueduct that spanned a French river so far down it was more like a gleaming root than water. Charles had taken photos of the foundations. When she'd come back—hair in a windy tangle, heart pumping—he'd said, "You know, they really shouldn't let people walk on this thing; a lot of that mortar in the big stones below is crumbly." He hadn't really grasped why she'd been upset he hadn't come to fetch her. "Men are a piece of work," says Mrs. Pritchard aloud.

Mr. Watson nods, and turns down a road, unpaved but smooth. Mrs. Pritchard can smell salt, and as they round a corner she sees the ocean, a copper slice in the sinking sun. In the center of the red bay is a factory, black in this light, a knot of tubes and pipes and smokestacks crouching on pylons.

Mr. Watson stops the car. The air is filled with the chattering of birds they cannot see. Brush crackles behind the trees. Before them is a wide, paved lot whose concrete has split with sprouting palms.

"What is it?" Mrs. Pritchard asks.

"An old bauxite plant. They found cheaper labor in the Soviet Union," Mr. Watson says. He gets out and leans against the hood.

Mrs. Pritchard also leans on the hood, not quite as casually. The engine, as it cools, makes small pops and rattles. Mr. Watson lights a cigarette. Its tip glows the same color as the water.

It is nearing total darkness now and Mrs. Pritchard listens to the slap of water on the pylons of the abandoned plant. In the dimness, it is impossible to see the sharp edges of Mr. Watson's face. She realizes she hasn't thought once about her illness since the car ride began. It's as if direct contact with him keeps it at bay. She makes a guess and asks him if he likes opera.

He waits a moment then says yes. He turns toward her; that much she can see in the deepening dark. "You hold your head like a singer," he says.

She says, "Yes, of course, that's what it is, isn't it. Keeping the throat clear. You have it, too."

They are silent for a few moments. Mrs. Pritchard thinks if they were speaking in French, they would nonetheless use the formal address, even after the intimacy gained through mutual loss of temper. Despite her curiosity, there's just so much territory they can cover. "How long have you worked at the Black Moon?"

"Four years. Three for the man before Carrothers, one for her. He was Rhodesian, too."

"Is she going to fire you?" Mrs. Pritchard asks.

"Soon," says Mr. Watson. "She doesn't like staff with backbone."

"What will you do then?" she asks, looking out at the blackening sky. It is the time sharks feed, the worst time of day to swim, although the water, for the first time in her stay, looks inviting.

"I used to work here," he says, pointing at the plant with the hand that holds the cigarette as if that answered the question. "There's McDonalds, Kentucky Fried."

"Do you want to stay in Jamaica?" she asks, feeling that flight might be an answer.

"And go where? America?" he says. "Would you like to sponsor me for a green card? And what would I do when I got there? Start training as an opera singer? Drive a cab and find a gun at my neck one night? When people are crazy on the island, at least I understand it." He slouches lower. "It's time to get you to the hotel, Mrs. Pritchard."

Mrs. Pritchard & Mr. Watson

She climbs back in the car. It seems to Mrs. Pritchard they are both tired. Her body aches. Her hands sit in small fists in her lap. As they turn back on the drive to the main road, animals hoot and dart in the brush. She imagines her white room. She will call Charles to tell him she is coming home.

A spray of bats bursts from the trees, histrionic, spiky. "Vampire bats," he says. Not for effect, just a fact. She knows, anyway, that their prey is cattle not humans. Mr. Watson's profile is smooth and closed. He is heading back to the hotel and it sits on his shoulders the way Mrs. Pritchard's illness sits on hers.

On the main road, a car with its headlights on high seems to race toward them. Mrs. Pritchard thinks first the car is in the other lane. Then she sees it is coming straight at them. The Jamaican game he described to her, the reason he insisted on driving. She hears a radio turned very loud, a bright confusion of sound streaming from the other car and Mr. Watson whispering, "Damn fools! Damn fools!" The car is getting closer. It is a station wagon with a spiraled crack across its windshield. It is close enough to see the driver and his load of passengers. She's aware of many elbows, raised like wings to shield faces. The headlights are very near and impossibly white, so hot she has to shut her eyes. Dominic is still whispering, but she can't make out the words. All she can hear is the fast and heavy knocking of her blood in her temples, her chest, her wrists. She doesn't want to know what he will do. With this, she feels a high clean lightness in her body, an upward rush with no fear. She is in his hands.